WHAT TO EXPECT WHEN YOUR DEMON SLAYER IS EXPECTING

ANGIE FOX

MIB
Moose Island Books

ALSO BY ANGIE FOX

THE ACCIDENTAL DEMON SLAYER SERIES

The Accidental Demon Slayer

The Dangerous Book for Demon Slayers

A Tale of Two Demon Slayers

The Last of the Demon Slayers

My Big Fat Demon Slayer Wedding

Beverly Hills Demon Slayer

Night of the Living Demon Slayer

What to Expect When Your Demon Slayer is Expecting

THE SOUTHERN GHOST HUNTER SERIES

Southern Spirits

The Skeleton in the Closet

The Haunted Heist

Deader Homes & Gardens

Sweet Tea and Spirits

Murder on the Sugarland Express

SHORT STORY COLLECTIONS:

A Little Night Magic: A collection of Southern Ghost Hunter and
Accidental Demon Slayer short stories

What to Expect WHEN YOUR DEMON SLAYER Is Expecting

NEW YORK TIMES BESTSELLING AUTHOR

ANGIE FOX

Copyright © 2018 by Angie Fox

This edition published by arrangement with Moose Island Books.

What to Expect When Your Demon Slayer is Expecting

First Edition

ISBN: 978-1-939661-52-4

I

I've heard it said that *you can't go home again.* But as I steered my motorcycle down the Georgia highway, I realized that in my family, you can certainly go home, just not fifteen minutes late.

The cell phone in my coat pocket buzzed against my side.

Yes, I'd told my mother that we would be at her house by two o'clock.

It buzzed again, as if prodding me to drive faster.

Yes, I realized my mom had planned a birthday surprise for my husband, who rode with me. I'd suspected it the minute she'd asked me what griffins liked—as if the fact that he was a shapeshifter made him prefer a certain type of snack or beer or tie.

She'd better not have bought him a Southern-style bow tie.

My phone quit buzzing. For now, at least.

I glanced to the hunk of a man who rode next to me. Broad shoulders encased in a wicked black motorcycle jacket, sharp features under aviator sunglasses, and dimples deep and dark enough to inspire me in all kinds of naughty ways. Dimitri Kallinikos was all a girl could want, and more. He also treated me right, made me laugh, and he loved my dog as much as I did. What more could a girl ask for?

We were working our way back to my hometown after busting an evil voodoo cult in New Orleans. It was what we did. We fought evil in this world and sometimes into the next. Of course, my mom liked to remind me that just because I had a busy job didn't mean I couldn't stop home once in a while.

My life had certainly changed since I lit out of town after discovering I was a demon slayer.

For the most part, my non-magical, very proper adoptive parents had taken my career change in stride. At least after they'd gotten to know my hot-as-sin partner in all things good and right, and after he'd helped save us all from a demon invasion at our wedding.

My very proper mother had finally accepted that I liked leather and swords instead of golf polos and capris.

The phone began to buzz once more.

God bless America.

I had to keep my focus on the road and my right hand on the throttle.

We were only another fifteen minutes out, but at this rate, it might as well be hours. I wasn't a huge fan of cell phones anyway, and this one was going to drive me nuts.

It rattled against my chest, as if poking me to ask: *Where are you?*

Fine. I'd put the question to rest, even if it meant taking longer to get there.

I held up an arm and signaled to the biker witches on all sides of me. They'd been with me in New Orleans and, well, my mom said I could bring some friends home.

I pointed to the exit up ahead and let it be known we'd be making a pit stop. A QuikTrip stood up ahead, much like the one I'd stopped at while fleeing town in the first place.

One point for déjà vu.

At least there was no hell spawn chasing us this time. Well, none that we knew of at least. These things did tend to pop up when I least expected them.

The witches gunned their engines up the exit ramp, and I couldn't help but smile when an immense white dragon sailed overhead, leaving me briefly in his shadow.

Flappy had really grown up in the two years since I'd found him as an egg. He hunted on his own. He was great at keeping an eye out for danger. The dragon landed on the roof of the gas station up ahead and gave a warbled shriek.

Good thing he couldn't be seen or heard by non-magical folks. I doubted my mother would want him near her prized rosebushes.

We pulled into the far end of the lot, near a large field, and for a moment I felt as if I were outside Jasper in the middle of the night, clinging to my grandmother's back, terrified of my first time on a motorcycle and the imps that were chasing me. Imps were petty annoyances compared to the demons I had faced since.

Pirate had tried to face down the imps and nearly been torn to ribbons in the process. I wondered if he was thinking of them as we shut down our bikes. When the noise died down, I figured I'd ask, maybe offer him a little comfort. But the second Crazy Frieda's motorcycle stopped next to me, Pirate leapt out of the sidecar like a dog on fire.

"Wow, what a ride!" he said, shaking off in a move that involved his entire body. He turned in a circle. "I broke my new bug-eating record! I love it, they just fly right into your mouth, and you don't have to chase them or anything!"

"Let's not go there," I said.

Pirate was an energetic Jack Russell terrier, mostly white but with a dollop of brown on his back that wound up his neck and over one eye. Ever since I'd come into my powers, I'd been able to speak with my dog. In real sentences. In the beginning, I'd thought my new ability would enable me to at last crack the code on canine thoughts and behaviors. Now, I understood my dog mostly thought about bacon and beef jerky and pretty much any food besides the food I bought for him.

Frieda winked at me and patted her stacked blond hair, miraculously unmussed from her silver and white motorcycle helmet. "I'll go ahead and get the little baby a snack."

Frieda strolled for the main building, Pirate trotting at her side. "Dog treats," I called, "you know you want to be a good dog."

"I heard her say hot dog," Pirate remarked.

I pulled out my cell phone, unlocked it, and called my mother back.

"This user has a voicemail that has not been set up yet. Goodbye."

"Oh, for Pete's sake," I muttered.

It wasn't really a surprise. My mother had owned a cell phone for years, and she'd never bothered to set up her voicemail. She claimed it was because she was a Luddite, but I knew better. You couldn't navigate the shark tank that was the Atlanta socialite circle as effortlessly as Hillary Brown did if you were intimidated by something as simple as the settings menu on a phone.

I think she just wanted the freedom to be able to listen to who she wanted, when she wanted, on her own terms.

Now if only she would extend that courtesy to the rest of us.

Oh well. No doubt she'd call back soon. She was in a frenzy about something. Did I forget to tell her how many biker witches would be at her house for dinner tonight? There were only…

I glanced around and winced. Okay, there were a lot of us. At least ten witches at the front of the store, laughing and easing off their bikes. A dozen more filled every available gas pump, with others pulling up just to chat. Another handful by the field next to the station, hopefully not getting into any trouble. And even a witch named Bob, who pulled up last in a 1970s rocker cargo van with tinted windows and red and orange flames painted down the sides. A screaming skull decorated the back, and foam pool noodles crisscrossed the top, making a perfect dragon bed.

We'd needed something to haul the various spells and magical doodads we'd picked up from Ant Eater's family home in New Orleans. Plus, it was nice to give Flappy a break on long bike trips. He was still a growing dragon, after all.

The Red Skull coven was bigger and stronger than ever these days. Funny what settling down after thirty years on the run from a demon could do for your recruitment efforts.

I glanced over the laughing, back-slapping bikers. Good thing nothing could keep Hillary down for long, not even unexpected houseguests. If my mother didn't have enough canapés and artisanal cheese plates to go around twice, I'd know she'd been switched for a pod person.

I'd give it a minute before I tried to reach her again.

Grandma put down her Harley's kickstand and stretched her arms over her head with a groan, her silver snakehead ring glinting in the sunlight. She was an apple-shaped woman with iron gray hair who wore her leather chaps like she lived in them, which she pretty much did. The T-shirt under her black leather jacket read *Kiss My Asphalt*, and when she strolled over to me and clapped me on the back, I felt it down to my toes.

"How's it feel to be so close to your old stomping grounds, Lizzie?"

"A bit weird," I confessed. "Not bad. It's just not a place I belong anymore." Not the way I used to, anyhow.

Before I became the Demon Slayer of Dalea, I had been a teacher at Happy Hands Preschool. I'd lived alone in my condo with my perfectly normal, non-talking dog. I'd color-coded my daily planner and dreamed of dating the hot guy at my local gym.

Now I preferred leather to khaki, high heels to sensible oxfords, and the only matching belt I wore was the one that held my weapons.

Yeah, it was definitely a little strange to be back.

"I stopped to call my mom back," I told her, "but—"

A voice echoed across the parking lot. "Come on, I'll be fast!"

Grandma and I turned and watched as Creely and Ant Eater exited the QuikTrip, Ant Eater holding the bathroom key above her curly gray head. Ant Eater had several inches and probably fifty pounds on the engineering witch, and she used it to her advantage as she beelined for the toilet.

"Age before beauty, kid." She got in and shut the door behind her with a bang.

Creely scowled and pushed a lock of Kool-Aid red hair out of her face. "I know how many muffuletta sandwiches you packed away in your saddlebags," she yelled through the door. "You think I want to marinate in the aftermath of that?" She shook her head. "To hell with it, I've still got my Sneak spell. I'm finding a bush."

"I wish I'd had a Sneak spell on me the night we hauled ass out of here," Grandma mused as she watched Flappy rub his face over the T in QuikTrip vigorously enough to make it creak. "Remember what happened when we got to the one outside Jasper?"

How could I forget? "I remember the imps. And"—I turned to face my husband, who raised one eyebrow curiously at me—"I remember seeing you for the first time." I hadn't known about shapeshifters then, and Dimitri had been in his griffin form.

He smiled. "And did I impress you?"

"You just about scared the pants off me." He was beautiful as a griffin, with his tawny lion's fur and blue, purple, red and green feathers, but he was also as big as a truck. Seeing something like that dive-bombing you from above would scare anyone.

"From what I recall, we had to work up to the pantsless part," he teased in that irresistible Greek accent.

Before I could flirt back, Grandma said, "Remember how

6

you went on and on about missing out on dinner with Hot Guy?" She snorted out a laugh as she ambled toward the store. "You dodged a bullet there, babe."

"Hot guy?" Dimitri lost his smirk. "What hot guy?"

"Nobody, just some guy I met at the gym." Hot Ryan Harmon. Gosh, I hadn't thought about him in years.

Dimitri raised a brow. "How hot are we talking, here?"

I leaned in against Dimitri's chest and trailed a finger along the edge of his T-shirt. He'd dressed down from his usual GQ look for the ride back from New Orleans, and I was looking forward to peeling off his jeans and jacket and getting at the man underneath. *My* man.

"He didn't hold a candle to you," I said with total honesty.

Dimitri wound his arms around me and pulled me closer. "Well, naturally," he drawled. "I'm not asking because I'm nervous about the competition, I'm just curious. You don't talk about that time very much."

"There isn't much to say about it." Wasn't that the truth?

He leaned down and kissed me high on the cheek, then lower, close to my ear. I barely resisted the urge to moan. "Do you ever miss it?"

"Never," I murmured. "I'd rather look forward than back these days."

"Yeah? Me too." He pulled back far enough that I could see his grin. "I'm especially looking forward to getting you alone tonight in a room that doesn't share walls with the biker witches."

That sounded promising. "Oh really? What do you have in mind?"

Dimitri's hands slid down to the small of my back, spanning my waist in a firm hold as he hitched me a little tighter to his body. "Remember the last time in the shower?"

How could I forget? My feet had barely touched the ground. "Hmm, you may need to remind me," I teased.

He lowered his lips to my ear. "This time I want to try—"

"Hey! Lovebirds!"

Mother fricking H-E double hockey sticks. Nothing broke a moment faster than getting loudly called out by a woman who sounded like she'd been gargling with Jack Daniel's.

We broke apart and I looked over at Grandma, who stood outside the QuikTrip with a neon-blue Rooster Booster Freezoni in one hand.

"Save it and get on the horn to Hillary already," she called out. "Or this thing's gonna melt before we get there!"

If it wasn't one buzzkill, it was another. "Fine." I grabbed my phone and called my mom again.

This time she picked up immediately. "Lizzie!"

"Hey, Mom, what's going on?" Otherwise known as *what was so urgent it couldn't wait fifteen minutes?*

"Well, honey, I stopped by your house to put some fresh-cut roses in the foyer for when you arrived, but there's something…wrong here."

She sounded disconcerted. Hillary never let herself sound upset; it was practically against her religion to let on that everything wasn't perfect. My stomach tightened uneasily. "Wrong how?"

"There's this strange fog in the house—I'm trying to air it out, I've got all the windows open and the fans going, but it just isn't budging. I think we may have to have a heating and air-conditioning man come in." She clucked her tongue. "And on a Saturday, too."

Oh no. The last time I'd been in my condo, Grandma and I had just finished fighting off a demon named Xerxes in the bathroom. He'd tried to kill me, I'd blown him up—temporarily—and by the end of it the bathroom was a stinky, ashy mess. Heck, I'd melted imprints of my hands into the edge of the counter.

"Mom, you shouldn't be in there."

She laughed lightly. "Don't be silly, Lizzie. I drop by once a week to water the plants and freshen up the place."

She what? "I left it with demon ashes in the bathroom and blue vapor climbing the walls!"

"Oh, I hired a crew to clean that up."

She *what?* "Are they all right?"

"They came from a very highly recommended service," my mom assured me, completely missing the point. I'd have to find out who had shown up and check on the poor people.

"But this is different from that," she continued. "This smells like something's gone off in the fridge, only it's the whole house. And the fog is just—you know, it's almost like it's *sticky.*"

I clutched my phone so tight I was surprised I didn't break it. "Get out of there."

She sighed. "I am a bit light-headed."

"I mean it, Mom. Leave now. Just walk out of the house and keep walking. I'll meet you down the street."

Her voice was weaker when she spoke again. "Goodness, my legs feel funny. Like they don't even want to move."

"Mom!" I heard her stumble and hit the wall. Oh cripes, she wasn't going to make it out of there in time.

"Lizzie, do you hear that? It sounds like a man's voice, only...only far away. But I'm sure I locked the front door..."

"Cover your ears," I pleaded. "Try not to breathe too deep."

The phone line went crackly. For a moment I was sure I'd lost her, but then I heard movement. "Get out of there, Mom. Go!"

"I think..." Her voice was so soft I had to strain to make it out. "I think..."

A second later, the phone went dead.

9

2

I stared at my phone in shock, vaguely aware of voices around me—the murmur of Dimitri's low, intense concern, Grandma's questions getting closer and closer—but I couldn't move. I couldn't believe something like this was happening.

Only, I could.

I'd feared it from the beginning.

It was the reason I'd left town in the first place—to protect my family, to protect the kids I used to teach, heck, to protect the non-magical people in my life from any evil power or demented spooks or—

It was Pirate who snapped me out of it, prancing over from the QuikTrip with his tail held high. "Lizzie! Lizzie! They had a special, buy one get one free on Road Warrior Beefy Sticks!"

I cleared my throat. "That's great, buddy, but we've got to go."

I could fix this. I *had* to.

Pirate danced on his front two legs. "Aw, but, Lizzie, I haven't even watered the trees yet."

I raised my voice to the group. "Change of plans. We're

heading to my condo. My mom is there, and she's in big trouble."

Dimitri put a hand on my shoulder, sharing a little of the pure goodness and light of his griffin power with me. "Demon trouble?"

I placed my hand over his. "I don't know, but we don't have time to waste."

Grandma got to us in time to catch the last part of our conversation. "Hillary's at your old condo?" She groaned. "I knew we should have come back and burned that place down after last time. *Damn* it." She turned to the rest of the witches. "Saddle up, people! We've got places to be five minutes ago!"

"I'll ride with Flappy!" Pirate announced, then turned and shouted at the dragon, "Hey! Noble steed! Get down here; we've got a damsel in distress to rescue!" Flappy looked up from his impromptu scratching post, whuffled excitedly, and heaved himself into a glide down to the parking lot. The *T* he'd been rubbing against creaked ominously, then fell to the pavement below.

"No riding the dragon," I said, striding for my bike.

"Aw, Lizzie, why not?" Pirate asked, following.

"Because he doesn't know the way." I scooped Pirate up.

The last thing I needed right now was for people to look up in the air and see a levitating terrier speeding across the sky. Besides, I had a doggie carrier in my saddlebag. When Pirate was strapped to me, he got all the excitement and wind of the open road, and I knew he was safe.

Once I'd buckled him in, I swung my leg over my Harley.

We had *better* find my mom safe and sound. If we didn't...

I kicked the starter and my bike rumbled to life. My relationship with Mom had always been touchy, and I knew she wasn't enthusiastic about my new lifestyle, but when push came to shove, she always came through for me. And I needed to come through for her.

"Stay close to me," I murmured to Dimitri. He was my rock. My best friend.

"Just try to shake me." He leaned over and kissed me quickly, leaving me warmed down to my soul and almost breathless.

We surged onto the road like we'd been hit by a Bat out of Hell spell, going so far over the speed limit that I hoped we didn't run into any cops, because I wasn't stopping for anything.

Listening to my mother get pulled into something beyond her control had been horrifying. She didn't deserve that. No one did.

I mean, I was a demon slayer, I *thrived* on danger. I'd chosen this life. My mom had only chosen to care for me.

We'd better not find anything terrible at that condo.

We made it in record speed, roaring down my old street, noisy enough to wake the dead. We surrounded my mother's champagne-colored Mercedes S-Class parked demurely in the drive.

I rushed past it and up the stairs to the porch and tried the handle.

Locked.

"I've got a Lock Eater in my pocket, hang—" Grandma began as I leaned back for leverage and hammered my heel into the door, slamming it open "—or you could do that."

"Mom?" I stepped up to the foyer of my former home, one hand dropping to the switch stars on my utility belt. They were similar to Chinese throwing stars, only bigger, sharper, and way deadlier. They'd served me well in a lot of different ways since becoming a demon slayer, and I held one at the ready. Dimitri stood right behind me. He always had my back. I took a deep breath then stepped inside.

I felt...nothing. Nothing out of the ordinary. That was weird in and of itself.

Beige tile, beige walls. The welcome sign I'd bought at HomeGoods.

I'd expected the mist my mom had described.

Perhaps the smell of sulfur.

"Mom? Where are you?" I ventured farther into the condo, past the little table where I used to keep my purse and keys, which was now decorated with a bouquet of my mother's prized Black Dragon roses. They looked good.

On my right side, the door to the hallway bathroom lay open. I peered inside, almost afraid of what I would find, but again—there was nothing strange in there. No clinging fog, no blue smoke, not even my own charred handprints. Whoever Hillary had gotten to clean the place up, they'd been thorough.

Leave it to my mom.

Darn it, where *was* she? I checked out the living room as I walked by, but saw nothing. When I hit the kitchen, though—

"Mom!" I lowered my switch star and dropped to my knees beside her on the linoleum. She lay sprawled on the cold floor. I'd never seen her appear so still, so...dead.

A familiar strand of pink pearls wound around her neck, a gift from my dad on their thirtieth anniversary. I slipped two fingers under. She had a pulse.

I touched her chest.

She was breathing.

Thank God.

I grabbed her shoulder and shook her gently. "Mom?"

With her pale, straight hair and cream-colored complexion, she looked a little like an elegant ghost passed out on the floor.

"Hillary?" I tried, because nothing annoyed her faster than me using her first name. Not a stir, just strangely steady breaths.

I clung to that. If she was breathing, she was alive.

Pirate arrived, Frieda just a step behind him. "Oh no! Bacon-wrapped oyster woman!" At times, Pirate had trouble remembering people's names, but he never forgot the last thing they'd fed him. He licked her closest hand. "She doesn't look so good."

Frieda got down beside me, her silver bracelets jangling

musically. "Let me take a look, sugar." Frieda was the closest thing the coven had to a healing witch these days. She felt for Mom's pulse, checked beneath her eyelids, and then drew a purple crystal from her pocket. "Mild diagnostic spell," she said by way of explanation, never taking her eyes off my mom.

She ran the crystal over my mom, who wore what I called one of her "after Labor Day cheat suits," a tailored pantsuit of such a pale lavender that it just barely avoided being white. Mom would never be caught dead on the floor wearing a parka much less a designer pantsuit. I tried to steady my breath. It was no secret that we hadn't ever really gotten along, but she was still my mom and she loved me and she'd accepted me, and I needed her to wake up now.

Frieda shot me an apologetic look. "I'm not detecting anything abnormal."

Well, she was wrong. "I'll take a look." My slayer powers could be used to search out evil, whether it was hiding in a person, place, or thing. I'd used it to illuminate dark souls and help me grapple with demons of all sorts. Now I had to use it on my own mother. I was afraid of what I'd find.

I felt Dimitri close behind me, all his warmth and power ready to bolster mine. I could do this. *We* could do this. Heaven knew we'd done harder things.

I let my demon-slayer energy build inside me, growing from a tiny spark to an inferno. I fed it my worry, my fear for my mom, my love for the woman who'd raised me like her own; I let it build, fed the flames until my whole body felt on the verge of combustion. When I felt full to the point that I either had to release it or let it explode on its own, I focused my sight on Hillary and poured my energy into her body, scouring her soul for the reason behind her collapse.

There was definitely *something*, but it was faint, subtle…

I had no room to fail. I peered closer at it, but even as I focused my sight on one part of it, another bit faded away.

"No." I slammed my hand onto the floor. "There's

ANGIE FOX

something dark in there for sure, but I can't pin it down." I sat
back on my heels. "It's too faint. It's almost like it's wearing
camouflage." It didn't make sense. Demons were a lot of things,
but covert really wasn't in their playbook.

"We'll root it out," Grandma promised, more confident than
I felt. "Possession can happen to the best of us. Budge over,
Frieda." She joined us with a groan and an audible creaking in
her knees. "We got this," she assured me as she reached into her
leather satchel and pulled out a Smucker's jar.

This one was filled with a brackish green and brown liquid,
and when she opened it up, my nose promptly staged a revolt
and stopped working completely. My stomach sloshed
warningly, and I had to shut my eyes for a moment. "Strong
stuff," she said, "my favorite anti-demonic spell." She poured
the liquid around my mother like a halo, then splashed a little
on her jacket for good measure.

That should have woken her more than anything. I could
almost hear Hillary's cry of "Not my Dior!"

A thin purple haze rose up from the sludge.

"Is it working?" I demanded, even as it dissipated into the
air a moment later. It should have turned blue. "Where did it
go?" I pressed. Blue would have confirmed the presence of
a demon.

Grandma scowled and shook the jar. "What the hell? Is this
spell a dud?"

"I can't believe it," I said. The Red Skulls' spells always
worked. Someone could die if they didn't. Like my mother
could right now.

Grandma craned her head over her shoulder. "Ant Eater,
were you drunk when you put this one together?"

"Watch it, Gertie," Ant Eater snapped. "I could make this
spell drunk, high, blindfolded and with one hand tied behind my
back, and it would still turn out perfect."

I grabbed Grandma's jacket. "It doesn't matter," I said. "Get
another one."

16

She gave a hard nod and gently removed my hand. "Easy now," she instructed. Grandma reached into her satchel and grabbed another jar. "Everybody here cares about your mom," she said, unscrewing the lid.

Not as much as I did.

The spell hissed as she poured it out over the last one.

Purple smoke rose and dissipated the same as it did before. There was no flash of blue. No nothing.

"Sweet Jesus." Frieda whistled.

Ant Eater slapped her leg. "That doesn't make any sense. What kind of possession can beat one of our spells and keep Lizzie from nailing it down?"

Grandma glanced at me. "The strong kind." She sounded grim. "We need to get it under control before it's too late. I need fresh raccoon liver, stat."

"I've got some on my bike, let me go get it." Frieda pushed to her feet with more elegance than should be possible for a sixty-five-year-old woman in six-inch platform heels.

Dimitri stirred against my back. "I'm going to go run crowd control," he murmured. "We got a lot of stares from your old neighbors when we arrived. The last thing we need right now is civilians poking their noses in while the witches are working."

"Thanks," I said, squeezing his arm. Dimitri didn't have any ability with, or interest in witchcraft. He'd be more useful outside. "Try to keep Pirate and Flappy occupied too if you can." They didn't need to see this.

"It's going to be okay," he assured me.

I nodded. I really wanted to believe that.

He left, and Frieda returned a minute later with a bag full of ingredients.

"Raccoon liver," she said, pulling out a plastic baggie filled with a soft gray sludge. "I've got rattler gizzard in here too."

"Rattlesnakes don't have gizzards," I informed her.

"Oh, they do if you dig deep enough," she said blithely. "Now, let me see…"

She'd better know what she was doing.

Mom hadn't moved. Hadn't done so much as draw a deep breath. She looked small and helpless laid out on the floor. She'd lost a shoe, a satiny ballet-style flat that matched the suit.

I let the biker witches work, and as the concoction of various bits and pieces got more elaborate, I scooted back out of the way. I had to trust them. I mean, I always did.

My mom's shoe lay under the breakfast bar.

I drew it out. The witches would do better without me, I reasoned, clinging to the delicate ballet flat. It wasn't that I was a bad witch myself, it was just that—okay, fine, I *was* pretty bad at witchcraft. I had tried my hand at a few spells, but they never worked the way I intended. The last Lock Eater spell I'd made not only attacked the lock; it went after the whole door.

The biker witches' heads bobbed over my mom's prone form.

I didn't need to be good at witchcraft, not when I had my kickass demon-slaying powers going for me, but I worked on it anyway because I wanted every advantage I could get. I maintained my lack of spell casting finesse was part Grandma's fault, because what kind of recipe called for "a pinch of graveyard dirt" or "a dash of demon ash"?

She assured me I'd get better at it with practice. Therefore, I practiced. Dimitri and Pirate had learned to join Flappy outside back home during these sessions. It was safer for everyone that way.

"Here we go," Grandma announced.

I drew close, keeping to the outside of the circle. Mom still looked the same, only the witches had definitely made their mark. That suit was never going to be saved, and at this rate, I wasn't too sure about her hair, either. Hillary would be horrified if she could see herself.

I desperately wanted to see her horrified. I wanted her to wake up. I *needed* her to.

Grandma, Frieda, Ant Eater and a few others knelt around

my mom, laced their hands together and began to chant. The words weren't Latin—I didn't know what they meant—but they focused the coven's power on Hillary, exerting their control over whatever was possessing her.

I felt the rising power like static electricity against my skin, building up in the air until my hair had to be floating.

Bright blue sparks arced from witch to witch, like a Tesla coil gone into overdrive, then shot down into the center of my mom's body. She glowed with borrowed power, the sigils drawn on her skin and clothes lighting up like neon signs. It was beautiful magic and so powerful it almost took my breath away.

A few seconds later the sparks began to die down. After another minute, the light had faded entirely, and the sigils that had been painted wet and heavy on her were as dry as dust.

"Well…" I prodded.

Grandma sighed and leaned back, putting her weight onto her hands with a groan. "Well, that's shitty."

My heart sank. "It didn't work?"

"Oh, it worked, all right." She slapped the linoleum with one callused palm. "That's our strongest warding spell; it *always* works." She glanced around my kitchen, as if she could spot the trouble hovering over the breakfast bar or hiding next to the stove. "Trouble is, this ward's not gonna do the trick for long. Whatever the entity is that's possessing Hillary, it's dark, and it's incredibly powerful."

"How did we not spot this before?" I demanded.

"We were gone," Grandma shot back. She sighed. "I'm sorry, kid. I'm just frustrated." She leaned back on her heels. "Truth is it would have been easy for another demon to follow Xerxes over from the other side. We didn't exactly check before we left." She shot me an apologetic glance. "There are a dozen different kinds of hell spawn, but we were running, and we couldn't catch the dog or get you on a bike, and we were flat out of time. I was a little off my game." She sighed. "Xerxes was the only baddie I warded against on the way out."

ANGIE FOX

I felt cold. "You mean it's been here all that time? Why not go after my mom sooner?"

"I can't say, but I can tell you this." She sighed tiredly. "Even with our strongest spell, we've got a max of three days to get whatever it is out of Hillary before it takes her over completely. After that, she's gone."

3

When I was a kid and objecting for one reason or another about having to do my homework or practicing the piano, Hillary would tell me, "Idle hands are the devil's playthings."

I didn't know whether that was meant to be motivational or scary—at the time it was neither, since I didn't realize that devils were real back then—but if she could see all the activity going on around her now, she'd be impressed. The witches weren't taking any prisoners when it came to securing the condo or my mom.

It was the least they could do, considering Grandma's failure to ward the place when we left. I tamped down my anger as Ant Eater barked out orders and the witches scurried to follow them. It would do no good to point fingers now. Grandma had done the best she could at the time. Heaven knew I hadn't always been the ideal kick-ass demon slayer, especially when under life-and-death pressure.

We just couldn't afford to make any mistakes now.

Ant Eater organized the witches into squads, each one handling a different room and festooning them with colorful and occasionally noisy defensive spells. Creely was looking at ceiling angles and taking measurements and muttering about "overspill," whatever that was—maybe she was trying to make sure the neighbors on either side didn't end up accidentally whiffing any spell residue.

I stayed with Grandma and Frieda, watching over Mom. We moved her upstairs to my old room—it was lucky that Hillary was light—and laid her down on my white ruffled bed. Grandma and Frieda conferred on ways to boost the defensive spell already on her. And I was frankly feeling pretty useless. I'd reached out again, trying to feel something, anything with my awesome demon-slayer powers, but I might as well have been using them to predict the weather. I had nothing.

"Oh, Mom," I murmured, the bed dipping as I sat next to her.

All the time I was growing up, it felt like Mom was completely in control of my life. I'd hated it, and it had made me feel safe at the same time. Now to see her pale and lifeless, it was as if my anchor to what was right and good and sane had broken loose.

She was one of the busiest people I knew. Every moment was an elegant bustle from one perfectly planned event to the next, always taking care with presentation, always seeing and being seen. My wedding had proven a real trial for her once she realized that I wasn't going to be manipulated into doing everything according to her plans.

Finding out I was a demon slayer who hung out with a gang of biker witches and was marrying a shapeshifting griffin might have had a bit to do with it too.

This was the first time I could remember just seeing her… idle. Even her eyes were still beneath her eyelids, and that wasn't just because they'd been painted with a thick, gooey spell.

It was a relief when one of the witches called up the stairs, "Hey, Lizzie! Better go back up your husband. Looks like he's been cornered."

Cornered? Cornered by what?

"Watch Mom," I said to Frieda.

I ran downstairs, one hand hovering over a switch star, and rushed out onto the front porch before I realized it wasn't an emergency. Dimitri stood on the lowest step, blocking the stairs as best he could, arms crossed over his chest. It was his "I'm intimidating" pose, and it sent most people packing, but this time?

I glanced over his shoulder and sighed. He was cornered, all right. By an overly interested soccer mom whose hairspray skills put Frieda's to shame. Even as I watched, she extended one long-nailed hand and gently ran her fingertips down his forearm. "I didn't know deliverymen came in such an attractive package," she purred.

Dimitri wasn't impressed, and neither was I. "I'm not a messenger," he said, his tone firm.

She didn't get the hint.

"A handyman, then?" She smiled coyly. "I've got some pipes that could use an experienced hand. Or—" her eyes lit up "—where's your truck?"

On the one hand, I was relieved that Dimitri was all she was asking about. It meant one of the witches had cast a See Me Not spell over the bikes, not to mention the van. The spells were only good for inanimate objects at rest, but they could be surprisingly thorough.

On the other hand, I was intensely annoyed that Mrs. Hildebrand thought she could make a play for my husband. I popped up from behind him, beaming at her. "Hi, Jacqui!"

"Oh—oh my goodness, is that Lizzie Brown?" She placed her free hand on her chest. Dimitri removed the other one from his arm, but she put it right back on. The woman was an octopus. "Why, I haven't seen you for years, especially not in such a...*daring* getup. I thought you'd moved and sold the place! You surely needed the money, didn't you? That darling little job of yours can't pay much."

Aaand here we went, tumbling hip-deep into the pseudo-polite crap talking that was the way of the South. I put on my sweetest smile. "No, I've been too busy to sell." Not to mention that niggling concern about the demon smoke in the bathroom. "And by the way, it's Lizzie Brown-Kallinikos now." I beamed at my husband. "My husband, Dimitri, and I spend most of the year in California now."

Her smile had gone forced, and when Dimitri pushed her hand off this time, she didn't move it again. "Well, I see you married up, then."

"Actually," Dimitri interjected, "Lizzie is the head of the business. I just come with her to make sure her work happens as smoothly as possible. She's very in demand, after all."

"O-oh." Jacqui's aplomb had totally disintegrated by now, but she gathered herself as best she could. "And what is that business, if I may ask? Certainly not preschool."

It felt like preschool sometimes with the biker witches, but I didn't think she'd want to hear that.

"If I told you," I said with a wink, "I'd have to kill you. Bye now!" She finally took the hint, and a few moments later Dimitri and I were alone on the porch.

He shook his head ruefully. "She moved on me faster than a succubus in a Vegas nightclub. Southern hospitality, huh?"

"At its finest," I agreed.

"How's your mom?"

"Still unconscious." I rubbed my hands over my arms. "I've never had to fight a demon that's inside someone I care about. If and when I figure out what kind it is, how do I kill it without killing her?"

He took over the rubbing, and I instantly felt ten degrees hotter. It was impossible not to feel a little warm under the collar when my husband was touching me. "We'll figure it out. I promise."

"I hope." I blew out a breath. "If I knew which one I was facing, I'd have a better idea of what to do. I defeated the Earl of Hell, for crying out loud. But this one isn't showing itself. I don't know how to fight it."

"Yet," he amended. "You don't know how to fight it yet, but you will." He captured my gaze with his intense, rich brown eyes. "And you've got all of us here to help you out. We'll get hold of this thing and send it packing. I promise."

I hoped he was right. "You've got a lot of confidence in me."

He tilted my head up and kissed the very tip of my chin. "All completely deserved."

We might have gone on to give Jacqui a show right there on the porch if Grandma hadn't called out, "Lizzie! Hillary's awake!"

Thank the Lord.

My mom was indeed sitting upright on the bed by the time I clattered up the stairs, her legs straight out in front of her, most of her weight leaning back on her hands. She still seemed a little dazed, but when she saw me, she broke into a smile. "Lizzie, honey, you're here." Then she frowned. "Oh, darling, a hot pink bustier? With your complexion? It makes you look like you escaped from a circus."

I gave a sigh of relief. Yep, she was back all right. I sat down next to her and clasped her hand. "How do you feel?"

"Oh, fine, just fine. A little woozy, maybe. I've been cutting down on carbs," she said, patting my hand as she pulled away. "I might have overdone it, but it's nothing to worry about."

"What do you remember about what happened?"

She frowned. "I was on the phone with you," she said, speaking slowly as she worked to recall. "There was smoke," she added, as if remembering for the first time. "It wasn't my diet at all. Oh, that's a relief."

"Mom," I pressed.

She swallowed. "I was going to open the sliding back door to try to let the smoke out, but I don't...I don't think I made it that far. It smelled terrible"—she winced, remembering—"like rotten eggs."

"That could be any demon," Grandma said under her breath. "Did you feel rage?" she asked my mom hopefully. "Or maybe overly sad?"

Mom drew her brows together. Well, as much as she could. Her forehead didn't move much. "I…" She sat with her mouth open.

"Maybe you feel horny," Grandma prodded.

I shot her a look. "I doubt it's an incubus." We'd know if my mom had a sex demon inside her.

"It never hurts to ask." Grandma shrugged.

"I feel…" My mom drew a hand to her brow. "I feel…" She glanced up at us. "Tired."

Of course she did. The entire morning had been awful for her. Still, we needed more to go on.

"Did you see anything else?" I pressed my mom. "Did you hear anything?"

Mom touched her forehead. "There was a voice, but it was far away. I don't even know what it was saying."

"Think," Grandma urged.

"You said it was a male voice," I added, trying to help her remember.

"Did I?" Mom asked, with a bit too much uncertainty. "I don't know." She looked up at us. "It was like a dream."

What did *that* mean? I was about to ask when my mom finally turned her gaze on her pants. Her eyes went wide. "What the—what?" She was upright in a flash, ignoring the hangover effects of bending forward as she inspected her pants. "Jesus, Mary, Joseph and the mule, this is a two-thousand-dollar suit!"

I would point out that polished leather bustiers were easier to clean, but I decided to let that one slide.

"What did you do to me?" my mom demanded.

Grandma was already heading for the door. "I'll just let you two work that out," she said. Frieda was hot on her tail.

"You and me are about the same size, Hillary," Frieda said over her shoulder. "I'll bring up a few of my spares for you."

She chuckled. "You're probably gonna want to burn the stuff you're in."

"Burn it?" Hillary clutched at her blouse, which audibly crinkled under her hand. "I can't burn this suit! This is *Dior*."

Ha, I'd called that one. My sense of relief was quickly overruled by growing apprehension as my mother turned narrowing eyes on me. "Elizabeth Gertrude? Would you care to explain what's going on?"

I figured the best thing to do was just to go for it, like ripping a Band-Aid off. My mom wasn't one to dance around unpleasant subjects, and neither was I.

"Mom, the simplest explanation is that there was a demon lying in wait here in the condo—that was the smoke you saw and smelled. It attacked you while we were on the phone and tried to possess you. Grandma and the other witches contained it, but we haven't managed to cast it out yet. We have three days to figure out how to defeat it, or…" My voice trailed off, but I cleared my throat and powered ahead. "Or it's going to take you over completely. Apparently."

"Apparently?" My mom's voice was faint.

"Yes."

"I feel fine," she protested.

"I'm not sure you are," I said gently.

"I lied," she said, sitting down on the bed. "I feel like my head's been split open. And I can't think straight."

I joined her. "I'm sorry."

She nodded and then kept nodding. "Possessed, you say."

"Yeah."

"By a *demon*. Really?"

I sighed. "Yes. Well, we don't know what kind of demon it is exactly. There are nobility, like the Earl of Hell that I defeated when I first became a slayer. You have generals with legions—"

"Stop." She held up a hand. "Are you positive I'm not just shamefully drunk and dreaming this whole thing up?"

"I wish you were," I said truthfully. "But this is real life."

27

"Yes," she murmured. "It must be. There's no way I'd dream my own daughter in that wretched shade of pink."

"*Mom.*"

She winced. "Darling, just…if you could speak a bit more softly, please? My ears are ringing."

I took a deep breath and let it out slowly. Okay. I could handle this, I could chaperone my mom through this experience. "There's more. The witches laid a spell on you that will protect you for a while, but it required some very—let's say, some very *organic* ingredients." As in, made from organs. "Frieda wasn't joking about maybe burning this suit."

She arched one perfectly plucked eyebrow at me. "Lizzie, I have coaxed pinot noir stains out of a white chenille carpet. I refuse to be defeated by whatever this is."

In her defense, Hillary was a whiz when it came to getting stains out. She was the one who'd figured out how to turn my hair from lavender back to brown after I'd left a Color-Changing spell on for too long. Still, this was more than just a little red wine.

"Why don't you look at the rest of it before you decide?" I extemporized.

Hillary's mouth tightened. "What do you mean, the rest of it?"

There was no getting out of it now. I helped her off the bed —her legs were as wobbly as a newborn colt's—and into the tiny en suite bathroom that consisted of a toilet, sink, and economy-sized shower stall. There was a mirror set above the sink, and I held my breath as I flicked on the light.

Hillary stared wide-eyed at the mess that was her reflection. Her pale blond hair was streaked with red and gray, and a chunk of gristle stuck out over one ear. Her forehead, cheeks and chin were all smeared with the same substance, and as we watched, a piece of it flaked off, leaving a little pink hole in the glob above her eyes. Which—wow, Grandma had been thorough, even her eyelashes had a coating on them.

Her blouse and jacket looked like a serial-killer-inspired Jackson Pollock painting, and her pants weren't much better. Her shoes had escaped the worst of it. Her necklace as well, but that was about all that could be said.

"Some spell, huh?" I joked.

"Some spell," she said flatly. "Is this demon supposed to be so disgusted that it just flies out of me? Is that the idea?"

"Mom, I know it's disturbing, but these things really work." I met her eyes in the mirror. "It's gross, but it's saving your life."

"I'm not sure it's worth it."

I frowned. "Not funny."

"No," she said tiredly. "No, I suppose this isn't the time for that sort of humor. All right then." She straightened her spine, pulled out of my grasp, and turned to look at me. She had to lean on the sink a little to stay upright, but Hillary Brown the Unfazed was back in control.

"This is what we do next. You call your father, tell him to get the food in the fridge and dismiss the caterers, since I doubt we're going to be home in time for your husband's party."

Oh, good point. And *oh*, dang it, how was I going to explain all this to Cliff?

"Don't tell him anything about me being cursed or possessed or whatever it is, not until we can explain it in person, because I do *not* want to have to go through this twice. Your father is the type of man who nods and smiles over the phone and doesn't remember a word you said five minutes later."

"I'm sure he'd remember if we said you were possessed." It wasn't exactly like asking him to pick up milk on the way home from the store.

Her voice was as dry as dust. "You'd be amazed what a man can tune out after thirty-five years of marriage, Lizzie. It's better to break the news in person. Anyhow, I want a fresh pair of pants—*not* leather, if you please—and another shirt up here as soon as possible. Pastels are preferable, but I'll accept just about anything at this point."

That was good, because Frieda didn't really do pastels.

"My old clothes might fit," I offered. The white oxfords and khaki pants I wore to teach preschool weren't exactly my mom's style either, but they were closer than anything Frieda could whip up.

"Your clothes were stained by that awful blue smoke." Mom waved me off. "I'm sorry, but I had to toss them."

Good riddance, really.

"I'm fine," she insisted. "The only other thing I need right now is for you to leave the bathroom and make sure I've got total privacy for at least half an hour."

I could certainly do that, but... "Are you sure you're not sick or anything?"

The first time I had come under the fire of Red Skull magic, it made me nauseous. Come to think of it, I didn't feel very hot now. I brought a hand to my forehead. That didn't make any sense. I wasn't the one covered in raccoon liver, and it wasn't as if I hadn't seen this all before.

"Leave," she said, nudging me out of the bathroom and gently closing the door. "The only thing I need is a very, *very* long shower."

Fair enough.

※ 4 ※

I stayed in the bedroom to call my adoptive father. He deserved to hear about what had happened directly from me, and the last thing I needed for that conversation was a bunch of witches standing around giving me "advice" on how to break the news.

But as I stood looking out the window at the half-dozen Harleys parked on my lawn, I got to take the easy way out—the call went straight to Cliff's voicemail, which, I noticed, worked just fine for *him*.

"Hi, Dad, it's Lizzie." I tried to think of how to say it, trying to ignore the roiling in my gut. "Things have gotten a little... chaotic here at the condo, and we're not going to be able to make it home in time for the party. Mom says to cancel the caterers and put the food away for now. Mom is..."

I decided then and there that this wasn't the type of problem that could be explained adequately in a message. I dropped my head. "Mom will come back with us later today. Everything is fine." I hoped. "Totally fine," I stressed, as if saying it would make it true. "We'll see you soon."

I hung up with a sigh. That was almost as bad as one of my late-night excuse phone calls from when I was a teenager.

I ran a hand through my hair, which had a streak of red in it thanks to Creely. I'd never been a *bad girl*—not even close—but the few times I'd missed my curfew, Dad had let me hear about it.

I headed toward the bedroom door. I should give Mom her privacy. She had the shower going full blast, and with her beauty routine, she'd be in there for a while. It wasn't like I could help her by hovering. Still, I couldn't find it in myself to walk away.

I heard the clamor of the witches downstairs and felt the effect of their defensive spells crawling the walls and seeping through the floor. No doubt about it, they were being thorough.

So why did I feel like we should be doing more? I ran a hand along my old dresser, past the perfume bottles now clouded and gathering dust.

We'd left the door open and given a demon the perfect opportunity to waltz right through. Mom, in her desire to keep up the place, was the perfect victim. But one thing puzzled me: why now?

I leaned back against the dresser. Mom had been inside my condo many times. Why had the demon waited until I was almost here before it attacked my mom?

You'd think it would have happened when I was in Greece or in purgatory or anywhere else besides here.

Unless it was using my mom to lure me into something awful. But what? It had to show itself in order to get me, and as of then, it hadn't even given us a hint as to what kind it was or what it could do.

I gritted my teeth. I could think of one person who might be able to help me sort out the motives of evil, but my mentor, Rachmort, was in purgatory. He spent half the year down there ministering to lost souls. Grandma was in the weeds, same as me. And that left the last person on earth—or in spirit—that I wanted to ask.

I'd met a spirit in New Orleans on my last adventure, an old soul with a questionable agenda. He had haunted the tower room in Ant Eater's old family home, and it was sheer chance that I'd been the first person to encounter him there.

He'd wanted to 'talk' in the same way that Hannibal Lector chatted with Clarice. Or at least that was how it felt to me. The spirit never asked me for anything outright, but I had the feeling he was racking up points for a big favor later—one I'd dread.

I'd been glad to leave him behind and didn't relish the idea of getting back in touch, if I even knew how to do it. No way Grandma would help. She wanted nothing to do with him.

I felt a stirring at the edge of my consciousness and stood up straight. "Okay, that's weird," I said to no one in particular.

It felt like...him, a sickly sweet presence in the back of my mind.

I blew out a breath and strolled toward my bed. "It's fine," I reminded myself. It wasn't as if merely thinking about the spirit could summon him to my old bedroom.

Could it?

Oh, no, no, no...

I stood in the middle of the room, my gaze darting, attempting to detect any unnatural shadows. He liked to appear in shadow, even though he didn't need to look like anything at all. I didn't need to be dealing with him right now, or ever again.

His presence grew stronger in my mind.

I fisted my hands at my sides, closed my eyes, and focused on blocking it out. It had been a mistake to speak to him in New Orleans, and an even bigger mistake to accept his help. I wasn't going to do it again.

Hello, Elizabeth. He surged into my mind. His voice was smooth, cloying. And dang it—distance hadn't damped his power one bit.

Goose bumps shot up my arms. I'd been hoping the spirit would just go away, find somebody else to haunt. Our time together should have been over.

"You doing okay in there, Mom?" I called, desperate to talk to someone, anyone else. The shower was still going. No way she could hear me.

I'm glad you still think about me, he crooned like a lover.

I kept my spine straight and my tone firm. "Thinking is not calling. You need to get out of my head."

I like it here, he said simply.

I slammed my eyes shut. "You know how creepy that sounds."

This so-called "master presence" was not an entity to encourage. That was why I hadn't reached out to him in the first place. He had awesome power. And, yes, it had helped me defeat a crazed voodoo priest in New Orleans. But I didn't want this to become a habit.

My dear Elizabeth, the spirit said, chiding me, *you just asked for my help.*

"I did not." I'd considered it, and he'd barged in before I could put two thoughts together.

You called me here, he said, as if correcting a child.

I pressed my lips together. He was right, but his barging into my mind made me realize what a mistake it had been to even think of him in the first place.

I'd figure out another way. The biker witches were already working on it. "You need to leave me alone now," I said, pressing my backside against the dresser, wishing for once that one of the biker witches would come up and barge in on me. "Goodbye."

I've heard that before, but if I had left you alone in New Orleans, you and everyone you love would be Mamma Pade's undead minions right now.

I locked my eyes on the framed college diploma on the wall next to my old bed. I could hardly remember a time when my life was as simple as going to school, getting good grades, and hanging out in the student union after class. "We would have found a way out of that cemetery without your help."

Would you, really? It's cute of you to say, but you don't truly believe it.

His voice lowered a little, taking on a more intimate quality that made me want to cringe away. *You can't lie to me, Elizabeth. You shouldn't even try.*

I shoved off the dresser. "What do you want now?" I demanded, spinning in a circle, wishing I could at least see his face, look him in the eye. I had to stay on the offensive, verbally and emotionally, if I was going to best this creep.

I want to help you. Just like before.

I let out a huff.

Just like always, he added, sugary sweet.

There was a weird possessiveness to his tone that bothered me. It wasn't the only thing.

"I know you have an angle," I told him.

He didn't deny it.

I walked to the window. "What makes you think we need your help? I've got a coven of witches working flat out to figure this out, not to mention my own abilities." I turned to face the empty room. "And there are plenty of other people I'd turn to for help before I ever asked you." People like my mentor, Zebediah Rachmort, who was a powerful necromancer and a leading expert on demonic powers.

He's in purgatory, and you're hiding upstairs.

Way to cut right to the bone. My lips contorted in an involuntary snarl. "If all you're going to do is insult me, you can—"

A shadow passed over the room.

Elizabeth, really. Don't let your human urge to fight get in the way. The spirit's voice became a bit warmer, more wheedling. *I can be useful in ways you can't even imagine.*

I didn't want to imagine them, either.

But you should, he almost purred. The shadows in the corners of the room deepened.

I turned on the bedside lamp.

It wasn't enough.

Imagine, with your raw power and my vast knowledge at your fingertips, you could be more than just a demon slayer. Much more. He spoke more persuasively than the snake in the Garden of Eden.

And we all knew how that story had turned out.

"I'm not interested," I said, striding forward, "and I'm not going to be." Mom's shower still blasted, and the spirit was right on one count—I wasn't doing her any favors hiding out up here. "You should hightail it back to New Orleans," I said, heading for the door, "and find someone else to follow around."

I heard him chuckle as I turned the knob.

I might leave you be if something more interesting came around, he offered. *But, Elizabeth, there is very little in this world more interesting to me than you right now.*

Oookay, the creepiness had just increased by a factor of ten.

I swung the door open, keeping my back straight and my motions confident. "The harder you push," I said, bracing a hand on the jamb, "the less I'm going to want anything to do with you."

Oh, my dear, he said, far too delighted, *we'll see how you feel tomorrow.*

I turned my back and walked out.

He didn't follow.

With blessed relief, I felt the spirit fade into my subconscious. Good riddance.

I breathed easier with every step I took down my beige-carpeted stairs. Then I was annoyed at myself for being relieved. I was a take-no-prisoners demon slayer who didn't crumble at the first sign of trouble.

I was powerful, in control.

My stomach gurgled uncomfortably. I was hungry.

Maybe if I took care of myself, I could come at this with a new perspective. I hadn't eaten since breakfast, and that was six hours in the rearview mirror at this point.

I walked down into the kitchen, dodging witches and skirting around spell jars. The ubiquitous Smucker's containers lined the walls three jars deep, but none of the spells inside seemed particularly energized. Some spells seemed to sense when they were getting close to action, even before they were let loose. I'd seen them writhe, wriggle and quiver in anticipation of doing what they were made to do, but these were all fairly placid.

More strangeness.

I opened my old cupboard door and looked for something to snack on. An old can of tuna, ugh, and that peanut butter was definitely past its prime. Maybe I had a—aha!

I grabbed the box of saltines and pulled it open. The crackers had to be stale, but that didn't matter. They pretty much tasted like cardboard from the get-go. I nibbled on a few, and my stomach settled gratefully.

"Lizzie? What are you working on in here?"

I whirled around to face Grandma, who was looking at me like I was the strange one. "Nothing!" Other than accidentally summoning questionable spirits from the Big Easy. "I was just hungry," I said after swallowing my overly dry mouthful of cracker. And maybe stress eating. Sue me. I had a reason. "Did you find anything useful in the house?"

She rolled her eyes. "What, like a convenient portal with a sign on it saying 'Home of Fred the Demon' on it?"

"I'm sorry I got a little impatient before," I said, handing her the box of saltines.

Grandma shrugged and grabbed a small mountain of crackers. She popped the entire thing in her mouth, washing them down with a swig of Jack Daniel's from a little flask inside her leather vest.

"I get that you're frustrated," she said, wiping her mouth with the back of her hand. "The place was brimful of demonic smoke that even Hillary could see, and now…nothing."

I refused to believe it. "You had to have found *something*."

Grandma frowned. "We're no closer to figuring out which demon has your mom than we were when we first got here." She sighed as she capped her flask. "That's strange in and of itself." Her feather earrings swayed as she shook her head.

"Objects and places, they have a memory of sorts. They carry the residue of things that were done in them for—years, sometimes. It shouldn't be so damn difficult to tap into a baddie that made its move today."

My heart sank a little. "But it is."

"Yeah, it is. Even for Ant Eater." She drew closer. "Don't tell her I said this, but when it comes to spells that pack a punch, she's second to none. You know that Glitterbug spell of hers that she used as a barrier to protect the house in New Orleans?"

I remembered that spell. It had been beautiful and full of power.

"She set it off here, and it just fizzled."

That wasn't good. I set the box of crackers down on the table, my heart rate picking up a little. If the coven really wasn't getting anywhere... "There might be another avenue we could try for information."

Grandma perked up. "Spill it."

I took a deep breath. "The spirit I met in New Orleans offered his help."

She looked blank for a moment then frowned so ferociously I thought her eyebrows were going to fuse in the middle of her forehead. "He's still there? What the hell, I thought you left him behind!"

"I did too." Except I knew I hadn't, not really. "But he's here, and he says he can help."

"Don't you listen to a single word that comes out of that thing's insubstantial mouth. I mean it, Lizzie." She pointed a silver-ringed finger at me when I opened my mouth to talk. "We don't know enough about it to want to give it any kind of leverage over you. Heck, you don't even know its name, do you?"

"No." All I really knew for certain that it had been haunting a Ouija board before it found me, and that it knew things that had helped me in the past. "It's not ideal," I admitted.

"Ha." Grandma shook her head. "*Not ideal.*" She drew closer, her eyes boring into mine. "You give an inch, a thing like this might take a mile and then take another lap for good measure. You don't want to be indebted to it. Whatever it's offering you, you should tell it no deal and move on."

She was right. I knew she was right—the last thing I needed right now was to complicate things by using a supernatural consultant that I didn't know how to shake yet. As soon as my mom was safe, we'd have to work on getting the spirit out of my head for good. "I got it. But what else can we do?"

Grandma drew back. "That's the question, ain't it?" She hooked her hands into the belt of her jeans. "We've still got options. Come on up to the living room and we'll talk about it."

We passed Frieda on the way, who had a big bundle of clothes tucked under one arm and a cheery smile on her creased face. "I thought I'd bring your mama some variety," she said to me as she headed for the stairs. "Does she wear thongs?"

"Not even the sandals," I said. Frieda just laughed.

We dodged two more witches on the way to the living room, and Grandma motioned me toward the couch. "Sit down and put your feet up, Lizzie. You look tired."

I did feel a little beat. I settled in on the couch, but before I could get too comfortable, Grandma squished in on one side of me and Creely squeezed in on the other. "Okay"—Creely leaned forward as Ant Eater planted herself on the green cushion that had once been Pirate's "—the working theory is that your mother was especially open to possession because she had no defenses in place, not even an Evil Eye charm bracelet. This was obviously an oversight on our part."

"On my part especially," Grandma owned. "I should've warded her after the wedding, but it slipped my mind."

"I blame the keg of Pabst Blue Ribbon," Ant Eater said, crossing her legs on the floor and thoroughly squishing Pirate's dog bed. "We never should have tripled the alcohol content with that Spell of Plenty. I've never had a worse hangover in my damn life."

"At any rate," Creely continued, "the task in front of us now is twofold: one, we've got to get the demon out of your mom, and two, we've got to set up a defensive spell powerful enough to ward her against any other attempts at possession. To do that, we're gonna have to brew up a mega spell." She spread her arms apart in a "like, really big" gesture. "We need a Praesidium spell."

Ant Eater let out a low whistle.

I'd never heard of it before. Admittedly, I'd never heard of a lot of spells before, but if this was as powerful as Creely said, then I wondered why no one had mentioned it to me earlier. "What does this spell do, exactly?"

"Think of it like a mini-magical atomic bomb," Grandma said. "You cast it, and the big boom gets this demon out, then afterward nothing else can grow there because there's nothing for it to latch onto."

In this case, the cure sounded as bad as the disease. "You make it seem like you're going to incinerate my mom's psyche."

"The good stays; the bad is annihilated," Creely explained. "It'll make your mom feel good. It'll help her tighten her grasp on her own spirit and purpose."

"Like a butt lift for the soul," Ant Eater added with a cackle.

"If you're into that type of thing," Creely teased.

"But it won't change her," I clarified.

"No," Creely said, growing serious again. "What makes Hillary Hillary is there to stay. Still, it's a hell of a spell, Lizzie. It can ward off all kinds of demons and soul suckers for years, even decades."

That couldn't be all. "What's the catch?" I asked. Because if it was really that easy, then I expected that the Red Skulls would be casting this spell left, right, and center.

Grandma scratched her nose while she tried to think of a way to tell me a piece of news I probably didn't want to hear.

"It's not a catch," she said, "as much as a challenge." She glanced at Creely. "The Praesidium spell is some of the highest magic an earth witch can cast, and it takes a lot of things *from* the earth to power it. Powerful herbs, rare flowers, stuff like that."

"And we've got most of it," Creely said, brushing her bright red hair back from her face. "What we don't have we should be able to rustle up pretty easily, with a little bit of outreach. Except for one thing. The kicker, so to speak."

"Ugh." Ant Eater shook her head. "That. I've been trying to forget about *that*."

I was tired of being talked around. "Spill it," I ordered. This was for my *mom*; I would get a lift on a fairy path and go halfway around the world if I needed to if it meant saving her life. "What do we need?"

"Moly," Ant Eater said grimly. "We need moly. And there's no tougher herb to get your hands on these days, especially in America. The last time I saw any of it growing here was in the seventies." She brought a hand to her mouth. "I lost a tooth getting it."

"You could have lost your life," Grandma said. "You know neither one of us can go after it again. We're cursed not to even see it."

"But Lizzie can go," Creely suggested.

"She could," Grandma said without relish. She turned her gaze on me. "You'd have to be very, very careful."

"And brave," Creely said.

"And fireproof," Ant Eater added, with a grin and a flash of gold tooth.

"Oh, geez." I had gotten myself into a lot of scrapes with the witches, but this seemed like the next level.

"Are you up for it?" Ant Eater prodded.

"I am," I said, sounding more confident than I felt.

Holy moly.

≈ 5 ≈

"When you say fireproof…" I began.
     I suddenly had visions of a dragon-shaped plant belching flames at me. And not the cute, Flappy kind. "Are you telling me that this moly stuff can set people on fire?"

"No, no," Grandma assured me. "Well, not exactly," she amended. "From what I understand, moly itself is pretty harmless. Sure, it's hard to dig up, and it can literally eat right through your hands if you get its juices on you, but nothing special."

"Oh, sure. Of course not," I said. Just when I thought I'd gotten used to the biker witches…

Grandma ignored my trepidation. "It's just that moly…well, it attracts a certain *type*, if you know what I mean."

"No," I said flatly. "I have no frickin' clue what you mean. Spell it out for me." I was going to work my butt off to save my mom, but I wouldn't charge headlong into a situation where not knowing all the details could get someone hurt.

Creely huffed impatiently. "Moly is an incredibly powerful, supernaturally attractive substance. Most of the plants we use in spells are pretty normal, the kind of thing you might find in a

43

garden or greenhouse. Moly, though…legend says it grew out of the blood of a giant. You know about Odysseus?"

I frowned, trying to remember back to eleventh-grade English class. "He's the guy who got lost for a decade after the Trojan War, right?"

"Yep, that genius." Creely's wallet chain clinked as she leaned forward. "He and his crew tangled with a witch named Circe, and she turned all of his sailors into pigs. She would have done the same thing to Odysseus if a god hadn't given him moly beforehand."

I could go for that. If the legend was true. "This stuff really works, huh?"

"It works like a charm," Ant Eater drawled. "It's just usually protected by vicious supernatural predators or crazy-ass witches who should put a damn sign up if they don't want you accidentally crushing their singing begonias."

Grandma rolled her eyes. "Let's not rehash that again. We have to figure out where to get some moly. Anyone hear about any giants that have been taken out recently?"

My kitchen contained at least seven witches, who all stopped what they were doing to consider the question.

A male witch named Bob stroked his gray goatee. "What about that earthquake in Belize?"

A purple-haired witch next to him gave a dismissive wave. "That was the Martinez Coven trying to brew up a batch of magic tequila. No hangovers, but highly explosive."

"Anybody know any giants?" asked the short, stout witch spelling the cabinet next to my sink.

There *had* to be an easier way to find this stuff than tracking down dead giants. I pushed to my feet. "I need to talk to Dimitri."

He was still outside, doing his best to remind Flappy that cars were *not* for bouncing on while trying to keep Pirate from arguing that of *course* they were, they were *there*, weren't they? I took in the gashes in the paint on the top of Hillary's sedan and winced. At least she had top-of-the-line insurance. "You boys have been keeping busy, I see."

Dimitri didn't look amused. "This is the nosiest neighborhood ever. I swear every five minutes someone new comes along who just *has* to introduce themselves to me and ask about you. I've had to turn away three pitchers of sweet tea and a Coca-Cola cake to keep them from barging into the condo."

"And not a single treat for me!" Pirate added. "No Schnickerpoodles or Paw Lickin' Chicken Bites. It's like they don't even remember me, Lizzie! Where's the love? Where's *my* cake?"

"Now that we're home and in a stable environment, I'm starting you back on Healthy Lite dog chow," I informed him.

"You see how I suffer?" he said to Flappy, who landed nearby and let out a warbling *yaark*.

While Pirate took his case of injustice to his dragon, I turned to Dimitri. "Have you ever heard of a plant called moly?"

He hummed thoughtfully. "Isn't that mythical?"

"Funny, coming from a griffin," I told him. He shot me an amused look. "We need it to make a protection spell for my mom, and apparently it's really hard to find. It's Greek, though." At least, I figured it had to be Greek. Odysseus was Greek, wasn't he? "Maybe we can ask your sisters?"

"They're not herbalists, but it's worth a try." Dimitri pulled his phone out of his back pocket and pressed a button. A female voice answered a moment later, and his face lit up. "Hey, Dyonne."

Diana and Dyonne were Dimitri's twin sisters and the whole reason we'd met in the first place. He'd needed a slayer to help him confront the demon Vald and rescue his sisters from a deadly curse. At the time, he'd told me he was helping me for *my* sake, that he was my protector. When it came out later that he wasn't, well...we'd had words. Loud, angry words.

Luckily, all that was in the past. I loved Dimitri, his sisters loved me, and he loved all of us. We were a regular old lovefest. If his sisters could help us, I knew they would.

Dimitri had to work to keep Dyonne on track. From what I could hear on the other line, she'd wanted to talk about his birthday, asking way too many questions.

At least I'd woken him up with a birthday surprise this morning.

"Yeah, moly." Dimitri pulled the phone away from his ear a moment later as his sister's voice went up an entire octave and several decibels. He shot me a wide-eyed glance. "I take it that's a no?"

The voice on the other end grew louder. He winced and held the phone out to me. "She wants to talk to you."

Ah, well. This should be interesting. "Hi, Dyonne."

"Lizzie! What on earth do you need moly for?"

"It's for my mom," I told her, not giving an inch. "You remember her from the wedding."

"Hillary? She cornered me with a hairstylist and gave me the updo from hell. Of course I remember her."

"Well, listen," I said, ignoring her tone. "My mom is in big trouble. We need the holy grail of anti-possession spells, and moly is the key ingredient. If you know where to find it, you've got to tell me."

Dyonne sighed heavily. "Oh, Lizzie, I'm sorry. I'd help if I could, but the Isle of Aeaea's been scoured clean for centuries. There probably hasn't been any moly growing there since the end of the Bronze Age. I went there to look for it myself back when I thought it might help Diana and I get out from under Vald's curse. There was nothing left but black rocks and old blood."

What a lovely image.

"I hate to be the one to tell you," Dyonne continued. "Even if I knew where to find moly, it's rumored to be incredibly dangerous to transport. The last person I heard of trying it dropped dead before he'd gone fifty feet."

This just got better and better. "Thanks," I said mechanically, and handed the phone back to Dimitri. He took it with a worried look, but I headed back inside before he could talk to me about it. Too much sympathy from my husband right now and I would break down, and my mom needed me to be strong.

Pirate walked with me, tail wagging. Oh, to be a dog.

I sat back down on the couch between arguing witches, pulled Pirate into my lap, and listened, hoping we could figure this out.

"—in Newfoundland," Ant Eater was saying. "It's just a rumor, but a rumor might be worth chasing down at this point."

Grandma shook her head. "We don't have the time. Even if it's true, we'll still have to fart around for days finding the thing, and we can't risk taking Hillary that far. If we jostle her too much, our holding spell won't be worth shit."

"We could consider making a deal," Creely said, and every other witch in the room made outraged noises. "Look, I don't like consorting with demons that way either, but they do *know* things," she defended herself. "If we get a lower-ranked soldier. If we're careful enough when we set the terms—"

"We can't trust a demon to abide by terms," Grandma scoffed. "Not with Lizzie in the mix."

Great. It was even *more* my fault that my mom couldn't kick her possession. Astonishingly, I felt a tear well up in the corner of my eye. I stiffened and carefully wiped it away. Yes, I cared, but I wasn't a crier. What was wrong with me?

Frieda broke the tension by strolling into the living room and pulling my mom behind her. "Ta-daa!" she announced, holding her hands out toward Hillary like she was a magician revealing her great new trick. "It suits her, huh?"

Sweet switch stars, I almost didn't recognize my own mother. She wore a leopard-print spandex bodysuit with an attached rhinestone belt sporting a huge cowgirl-style buckle. To top it off, a neon green bra peeked above the bodysuit's décolleté. She wore her own jewelry and shoes, no makeup, and an intensely peeved expression.

"Not a word," my mother ordered as the witches collectively drew a breath. "Not. One. Word."

"How about two words?" Ant Eater asked. "Such as *nice knocker*—"

"No!" Hillary held up a hand. "I am not having this conversation. I am not looking in the mirror. Now tell me what you are going to do to get me out of this mess."

Grandma stood to face her. "We've got a spell in mind that we think will work." She held up a hand before Hillary got too excited. "But it needs an ingredient that's hard to find. Real hard."

Frieda frowned. "What d'ya have in mind?"

"Moly," I said.

Her eyes widened. "Oh, for Praesidium?" She placed a hand on her hip and chewed her gum thoughtfully. "That's a good idea. You know what? You should ask Philippa about that."

There was a chorus of groans. "Setting aside the fact that she loathes us and has for decades, nobody even knows where Philippa the Strange is anymore," Ant Eater protested.

Frieda shrugged. "Oh, sure they do. I mean, *I* do. Battina kept in contact with her." Battina had been the coven's healing witch who was killed in a battle against a demon months ago. Frieda was doing her best to step up and take her place, and apparently that meant getting her address book too. "I guess she didn't want you all to know because of the whole—" she waved a hand indistinctly "—*thing* you had with her."

I didn't care about the witches' grudges. I only cared about my mom. "Where is this witch?"

"Philippa?" Frieda snapped her gum. "Oh, she's right here in Atlanta."

Ha! I set Pirate down and surged to my feet, newly energized. "Perfect, let's go talk to her!"

Frieda's smile slipped away. "What, you want…you want *me* to go talk to her? Oh no, I couldn't do that."

Yeah, well, I didn't have time for this. "You just said you know where she is."

Frieda grimaced and tucked a lock of blond hair behind her ear. "Well, sure, but she doesn't really like us Red Skulls. I tried reaching out to her a while back and got nothin'. She might give you a pass because you're a slayer, but me?" She shook her head. "I might as well stick a target on my forehead as go talk to Philippa the Strange."

I came over and gripped Frieda's skinny shoulders. "It's got to be you. You know what moly looks like, right? I have no idea! I wouldn't know if she was giving me a moly or a magic bean stalk."

"Well, you see, a bean stalk has pointed leaves—" Frieda began.

"Cut it," I told her.

"Lizzie's got a point," Grandma said. "Most of us, we wouldn't be able to see it anyway, not with Philippa's damn curse. You weren't a part of that mess, Frieda."

"That doesn't mean she likes me!" Frieda squeaked. "Philippa is really fussy, prim and proper, cup of tea and all that. She didn't even like Battina—they barely tolerated each other!"

"She thinks we're loud and uncouth," Ant Eater said, picking at her fingernails.

Gee, I wonder where Philippa had gotten that idea.

"You're my mom's best chance," I told Frieda. As far as I was concerned, it was nonnegotiable.

Hillary stayed silent, but reached out and took Frieda's hand. The yellow-haired witch glanced between us and sighed.

"Oh, fine. But you'd better be on your guard, Lizzie." She pointed a glossy pink nail at me. "I can't watch my butt and yours at the same time."

"I've been taking care of myself for a while, thank you," I told her.

"I'll come along as well," Dimitri said. "To provide extra security." He shared a glance with me that said *just try to stop me*, like he was expecting me to argue.

"That's perfect," I told him. I'd rather have Dimitri by my side than anyone else. I looked back at Frieda. First, we needed a plan. "Okay, what I'm hearing is that Philippa is the anti-Red Skull."

Frieda lowered her chin and gave me a look. "She hates our guts."

I nodded. "Then I know where to start."

❧ 6 ❧

"**D**id we really have to take the van?" Frieda protested, squirming in the passenger seat as if it was going to haul up and bite her.

"It's all part of the plan," I said, seeing her go a bit pale when we pulled up to the place I had in mind.

"What's going on?" She stared at me as I put the van into park and shut down the engine. "What do you think you're doing?"

Deep down, she knew. She had that same look Pirate got when I took him to the groomer's.

I opened my door first, while Frieda refused to move. I strolled over to the passenger side, half expecting her to lock the door. She rolled down the window instead.

I considered it progress. "Before we even think about talking to Philippa, we're both getting a makeover," I told her.

She gaped at the glass store windows in front of us, and at the blue sign on top that proudly proclaimed we were at the Gap. "No way in hell," she said, stiffening. "I look great the way I am." A rainbow of plastic bracelets jingled as she tossed out an arm. "Fabulous!"

"Think about it," I told her. "Philippa hates the Red Skulls. She thinks you're a bunch of rowdy biker chicks."

"And I'm proud of that," she shot back.

"Look," I said, placing both hands on the window ledge so she couldn't roll it up again, "first impressions count. Or in your case, second impressions. We need to show her we've changed. We've turned over a new leaf." I tapped a hand on the ledge. "We're even driving a van!"

Sure, it had flames down the side and a dragon's nest on top, but it was progress.

Frieda looked like she'd swallowed a lemon.

Dimitri smiled from where he lounged on the back bench seat. "I'll wait in here," he said, feeding Pirate a beef jerky treat.

Spoken like a man on a shopping trip.

"I'll see what they have," Frieda said, reluctantly opening her door. "But I'm not wearing plaid."

"Think of it as a costume," I said, tossing a wink to Dimitri as I led a stiff-legged Frieda into the store.

Dimitri had already dressed up. When I'd told him my plan, he'd changed into a pair of gray trousers and a black button-down shirt. I realized I had nothing to wear except for my leather and satin. I'd need a few things too.

We emerged a scant ten minutes later, with me in a gorgeous, flowered dress that flowed down to my new leather booties and Frieda wearing a denim shirt dress, minimal jewelry, and white tennis shoes. We'd used the dressing room mirror to comb down her blond bouffant into a sensible ponytail, and we'd added a simple tortoiseshell clip.

I gave a little spin, which Dimitri appreciated, while Frieda stumbled over the curb toward the van.

"I can't walk in these things," she said, picking up her feet like she wore alien shoes. "It's like my heels are sinking into the ground."

"You'll get used to it," I said, stuffing the bag with our

clothes and her mounds of jewelry into the back. "Thank you, by the way."

She gave a quick nod, her face drawn. "I'm doing it for your mamma," she vowed, as if I'd asked her to walk naked down the street during rush hour. "Now let's go see where Philippa is hiding."

⚜

I PULLED TO A STOP IN THE PARKING LOT AND JUST STARED FOR A moment. "The Atlanta Botanical Garden?"

Of all the spots an earth witch might hide, this was one I hadn't expected. It housed a lot of unique plants, true, but it was so *public*.

I shut down the van and drummed my fingers on the steering wheel.

I'd only been here a few times before, mostly to attend charity events Hillary had set up in the rose garden, but I remembered the layout of the place. The most isolated it ever got was the canopy walk, and that was still fairly crowded, especially over the weekend like it was now.

"Isn't it nice here at this time of year?" Frieda asked, fidgeting with her blond ponytail. "This is the kind of place that puts people in a good mood. I hope."

I shared a glance with Dimitri. Frieda's obvious nerves weren't doing the rest of us any favors.

Then again, Dimitri wasn't much better. He practically vibrated with pent-up energy as we set off on the sidewalk that led into the gardens.

"How can anyone live here permanently?" he asked. "Wouldn't they be discovered eventually?"

Frieda slowed her pace. "Not if she's warded to kingdom come and back," she said. "Philippa the Strange has always preferred plants to people, from what I understand."

"Lizzie! Lizzie, put me down. I need to sniff, *pronto!*" Pirate

53

wiggled vigorously in my arms and I worried he might fall free and brain himself. I set him down, and he immediately put his nose to the ground. "I bet I can find her! I've got a great nose for trouble."

"That's unfortunately true," I said dryly.

Dimitri lifted his sunglasses off and tucked them away. His handsome face appeared sharper than usual, his jaw tensed. "If she's as dangerous as she sounds, then you won't have any trouble finding her yourself, Lizzie."

That was *also* true. As a demon slayer, I had an instinct that led me *toward* danger rather than pushing me away from it. Still, Philippa the Strange wouldn't be actively trying to kill us, right?

My fingers danced over my switch stars. Right.

"People are looking at me," Frieda said, eyeing our fellow visitors. "Is my dress falling off?" She ran her hands over her torso. "It's so loose I can't tell."

"You look good," I assured her, "and nobody is even noticing you."

It had to be a first.

Just before we headed under the arches and into the gardens, I bent down and fixed an inky black Sneak spell to the back of Pirate's collar. They didn't allow dogs here, and the entire concept of *covert* didn't compute for him.

Once we'd entered the main path to the garden, I tried to relax and let my supernatural compass for danger take over. A formal rose garden bloomed to our left, with stone pathways and painted white trellises. To our right, a signpost stood before three different walking paths: home gardening, native plants, and the Japanese gardens.

I paused to consider.

In a few moments, I felt a subtle pull to the left, toward the Japanese garden.

"This way," I said.

Dimitri and Frieda flanked me on either side.

I'd been right. The garden was crowded today. We passed

several couples and families and didn't fetch a second look. It felt kind of strange, actually.

We passed a lovely lake, as well as a childrens' garden and play area, then we took a left at an immense tree that had to be hundreds of years old.

"Fairy fort," Frieda said when I'd stared a bit long.

I nodded to any fairies as we passed. Ant Eater had briefly dated a fairy and let us ride on the fairy paths. Aside from a haunted hotel, it had been *the* way to travel.

The dappled light filtering through the trees was almost meditative, the air cooler and sweeter than late summer in Atlanta had any business feeling. But I knew better than to let myself relax.

This was the calm before the storm.

"We're close," I told my friends.

We rounded the bend, and there it was—a sculpture like none I'd ever seen blocking our path.

It stood as tall as a house, the head and shoulders of a woman crafted entirely from plants, her hair a cascade of blue, yellow, and purple flowers. She held her arm over a fountain, allowing a trickle of water to flow from one gently cupped hand.

"This is too pretty to be it," Frieda remarked. She consulted a brochure she'd grabbed by the front gate. "*Earth Goddess* is what they call her."

I believed it. She stood on a base of pink limestone engraved with flowers and climbing vines.

"This is definitely the place." The danger seemed to be centered around the massive sculpture, but I didn't see anything that screamed "Look out!" in my mind.

Frieda stood motionless. "If there's a spell happening here, I don't feel it."

Dimitri's gaze darted over the small courtyard, as if he'd be able to unmask Philippa's magic by sheer will.

"Give me a second." I focused harder on the danger, but it was like looking through an old piece of wavy glass—I couldn't quite pin it down. "This feels like it did when I first discovered Mom on the floor of the condo." I couldn't get a lock on the presence swirling inside her, either.

"This is bad." Dimitri stepped in front of me, as if there was something to face, something to confront.

"Lizzie!" Pirate bounded past him before I could pull him back. "Look! A magic bunny!"

"What?" I stepped to the side and saw a rabbit on the grass, chewing placidly. I reached out with my slayer senses. It wasn't magic. "Don't worry about it, Pirate. It's just a regular old bunny that probably lives in the gardens—"

"No," Dimitri interjected, one of his hands creeping toward his back, where he kept an enchanted bronze knife hidden beneath his jacket. "Pirate's right. It wasn't there a second ago."

I gave it a second look, and even as I watched, the bunny hopped right up to the stone base of the sculpture—

And vanished inside it.

"Don't worry, Lizzie, I'll get that rascally rabbit!"

Before I could stop him, before I could even call his name, Pirate ran after the bunny, straight into the impenetrable base of the statue.

And with a horrified gasp, I watched him disappear too.

✣ 7 ✣

"**P**irate!" I ran toward the sculpture, grabbing a switch star from my utility belt. "Pirate!" I touched where he'd disappeared, and my hand sank right through the pink limestone.

I yanked it back out.

Was it an illusion? A portal?

"It felt like air." I turned to Frieda. "What is it?"

She whistled out a breath. "I knew Philippa was good, but wow. It's illusion magic, and I have no idea how it works."

Dimitri gritted his jaw. "Witches used to be put to death for it."

Yes, well, witches used to be killed for a lot of dumb reasons, but that was neither here nor there. My dog was gone, and he either couldn't hear me calling him or was ignoring me in favor of chasing that darn rabbit. "We have to go after him."

"We will," Frieda assured me, "but let's be Girl Scouts about it." She pulled a couple of Smucker's jars out of her purse and handed them over. "Deflector spell, Paralyzing spell. They're nice and fresh."

"Thanks." I stuffed them in the satchel on my utility belt and hoped they'd work for me. The look in Dimitri's eyes said the same thing. I didn't always have the best luck with biker witch magic.

My danger warning pinged hard and fast, urging me to step into whatever was on the other side of this sculpture. I straightened my back and squared my shoulders. "You ready?" I asked them.

"Unless you want me to lead the way," Dimitri said, obviously hoping I'd say yes.

"No, thanks." Pirate was my dog. I'd lead the charge.

I took a deep breath and stepped forward into the base of the sculpture, into the leg and torso of the earth goddess.

Energy buzzed on all sides of me, like a thousand tiny bees.

I had expected a hollow space inside the sculpture or maybe a swirling portal that would whisk me into another dimension.

Instead I stepped out into an immense, shaded grotto that put the regular Botanical Garden to shame. A small stone path led the way to a trickling fountain in the middle of the lush glade. Flowers bloomed in dazzling yellows, pinks, reds, and purples, the blossoms huge, the scents beautiful and rich.

Dimitri was right behind me. "You okay?" He placed his hands on my shoulders, as if he was glad to see me in one piece.

"I'm good," I said. "This place is—"

"Weird," Dimitri finished.

We scanned the foliage for any sign of life. "Pirate?" I called. "Where are you, buddy?"

Insects buzzed and frogs called, but Pirate gave no response.

Where could he be?

Frieda ran into the back of me. "Whoops! Are we in trouble?"

"Not yet," I told her, venturing forward to search the shadowy underbrush.

"Hooo-boy, look at this place!" she said. "Rosary pea,

monkshood…ooh, and you see those pretty columbines?" She pointed at a flowering blue and purple plant a few feet away. "Nice, right? But those suckers will stop your heart if you eat too much of the root."

I frowned. "Good to know." At least Pirate didn't like to eat plants. I took a step farther into the magic garden. "Come on, Pirate. You leave that bunny alone and I'll give you a Schnickerpoodle."

It was his favorite treat. And thanks to me confiscating a stack from a biker witch named Bob, who liked to feed them to Pirate like candy, I had a few in my utility belt. "Here's one," I taunted, pulling a slightly greasy, sort-of-peanut-buttery treat out of my side pocket.

Still, Pirate didn't appear.

This wasn't good.

"Um, Lizzie…" Frieda glanced around the grotto, her brow wrinkling. "I don't want to alarm you, but everything in this garden is poisonous. We're definitely on Philippa's turf."

Lovely. We'd been transported to a crazy witch's secret garden whose sole purpose was death and destruction. At least we'd found her.

"Let's stick together," Dimitri said grimly.

"Right," I said. We didn't want to lose anyone else.

My skin warmed as the emerald necklace between my breasts began to stir.

I exchanged a look with Dimitri as enchanted bronze snaked up my chest and down my torso. I tried not to grimace as it encircled me completely, forming a bronze corset.

"The more things change, the more they stay the same," I remarked.

Only this corset was much tighter than the one I'd ditched at the Gap. I peeked down my bodice and saw the teardrop-shaped jewel right between my breasts.

"There's no arguing with fate," Dimitri mused.

He ran a hand down my back and gently tapped my side with his fingernail. It made a *ting* sound. The breastplate covered me from my throat to my hips.

Back when we first met, Dimitri gave me an emerald pendant on a bronze chain. It was more than a piece of jewelry, though—it was spelled with defensive magic and transformed to become whatever I needed when I was in danger.

Apparently in this case, it thought I needed not to be able to bend over.

"Huh." I didn't usually get *this* much coverage from the necklace. The emerald gleamed brightly from the metal corset, a comfort and a warning all at once. "Okay. We'll stick together."

We still had to find my dog.

The grotto wasn't that large, but the foliage was thicker than shag carpet once you tried to leave the path. With Frieda cheerfully identifying all kinds of unpleasant plants—"Poison ivy! Belladonna! Water hemlock!"—it seemed safer not to risk tramping around in the undergrowth. But where was Pirate?

"Pirate!" I called, wishing I could spot even a glimpse of him. "Pirate, talk to me!" We walked around the fountain in the center of the place and toward the far side. My danger sense started going off like crazy, and I stopped in my tracks.

"What is it?" Dimitri drew his dagger.

"I'm not sure…" My senses homed in on a shady section right in front of us. A huge, thick-stalked plant rose almost ten feet into the air, crowned with a bright red flower that smelled suspiciously like rotting flesh. White orchids clustered at the base, and in front of them, growling under his breath, was—

"Pirate!" I ran forward, but slowed once I realized that the orchids were moving, swaying hypnotically back and forth in front of my dog. "Pirate?" He stood transfixed, clearly unhappy but just as clearly unable to do anything about it.

"Cobra orchids," Frieda whispered. "I've never seen this many in one place before."

Fudruckers. "Are they poisonous too?"

"Venomous, more likely," she said under her breath. Pirate wavered, and one of the little flowers hissed at him. "Yep, see the fangs?" Frieda prodded.

I did see the fangs. I didn't *want* to see them, but I did.

My poor dog.

"We don't want to startle 'em into striking," Frieda instructed. "This would be a good time for that Paralyzing spell, Lizzie."

"Right." I carefully drew a brown, murky spell from my belt and opened the top. The spell lumped sluggishly in the bottom of the jar—well, it was a *Paralyzing* spell; I'd have been suspicious if it had been jumping around. I took careful aim and tossed the contents at the cobra orchids.

Hisssss! Their striped hoods flared all at once. One of them turned to snap at Pirate, but wilted before it could reach him.

My dog shook his head like he was coming out of a nap. "Lizzie?"

I hurried to him and scooped him into my arms, awkwardly, thanks to the darn breastplate. "Pirate, sweetie! Are you okay?"

He yawned and snuggled close. "Oh sure! I was just following the magic bunny, but then I heard a new sound, and when I came over to check it out…" He tilted his head, ears flapping. "I stopped hearing anything at all."

"Oh, jeez." We needed to find Philippa and get the heck out of here. The scent of rot was getting stronger, and I resisted the urge to gag.

"Oooh, Lizzie." Pirate strained out of my grip. "Do you smell that?" He turned in a circle. "There's something delicious around here. Or at least something fun to roll in."

"There's something *disgusting* around here, and you—" All of a sudden my danger sense lit up. I reacted instinctively, grabbing Pirate and jumping backward. At the same time, the enormous red blossom of the plant just behind the orchids slammed down on the ground exactly where Pirate had been a moment ago.

"What the—" I had never seen a plant move that fast. I didn't have time to gape, either—two long, thick leaves shot out toward us, one of them striking at Dimitri while the other slashed at me. He parried with his knife while I turned my back and felt the leaf ricochet off my armor.

I put Pirate down fast and poured Frieda's defensive spell over him. It stuck to his fur like bubblegum, but it would help him evade attacks. "Stay back!" I shouted before quickly turning and throwing a switch star straight at the plant's heavy stalk. I expected to cut it cleanly in two.

Instead, my switch star bounced right back to me.

How in the heck did a weapon that could kill a demon get confounded by a murderous *plant*? I tried again, this time aiming for the flower itself.

Heavy green leaves closed around the bright red petals before my switch star could impact. As it came back to me, the flower reopened and lowered itself to face us. What I'd taken to be decorative fringes on the edges of the petals looked more like *fangs* at close range and would probably cut like them too.

Frieda cast a Molotov Cocktail spell into the heart of the blossom. Fire erupted, and I thought for sure the whole thing would go up in flames. Instead, the center of the flower belched out a torrent of thick, creamy sap, smothering the burn in a heartbeat. The sap rolled out of the blossom and down the stalk, effectively ending our chances of burning it.

The leaves lashed out again, and one of them caught me square in the stomach. It knocked me onto my back, and I had to roll quickly to the side to avoid being pinned by the next strike.

"Lizzie!" Dimitri turned to help me, which left him open to attack. The leaf struck at his head, leaving a bleeding gash across his cheekbone. Its next strike ripped the knife from his hand.

"Dimitri!" I tried to roll to my feet, but the flowing flower dress and the damn breastplate made getting up way harder than it should have been.

Frieda threw a spell I'd never seen before. It let loose a howling wind that tore the limp cobra orchids out by the roots, but the attacking plant just curled its leaves and petals in tight for the worst of the gust. As it faded, they shook themselves out and struck again.

"Eek!" Frieda tried to dance out of range of the leaves, another spell jar at the ready, but the plant swept down toward her feet and grabbed her ankle. She fell to the ground with a gasp, and the leaf began to reel her in. I reached for her, pulling another switch star even though the first one hadn't done any good.

With a low growl, my husband's familiar form morphed into an immense lion's body. The ground shook and eagle's wings sprouted from his back. Purple, blue, red and green feathers exploded into being, filling the air above us as he splayed his wings out like a shield. He leapt forward and pounced on the plant with a shrill battle cry.

The leaves closed protectively around the blossom, but Dimitri's sharp claws rent at it relentlessly even as his heavy weight bore the plant to the ground. It tried to bash him off with its leaves, but he knocked every attempt aside with his wings, clawing like a wild animal.

Bit by bit, the plant seemed to weaken. Thank heaven! Its stalk sagged farther toward the ground. We were winning! At this rate, Dimitri would end it in less than a minute.

Only Ant Eater had warned us about stepping on a single living flower. And we'd already decimated the cobra orchids.

"Dimitri," I called breathlessly, struggling to my feet.

He paused, one paw still raised. The plant quivered feebly beneath him. "Don't kill it," I said, helping Frieda to her feet. "Just—just sit on it for a moment, okay?"

"Honey." Frieda's shoulders sagged, and she fought for breath. "It tried to kill us first, remember?"

I shook my head. "It was acting on instinct, the way any creature would. If we kill it, we'll never get the chance to talk to Philippa."

I heard a low cackle behind us. "Good instincts, slayer."

Frieda and I whirled around to see a woman walking down the far side of the path toward us. She was tiny and round, and her face reminded me of a wrinkled winter apple. Her white hair flared out from her head like a crown, and she wore a brown pair of overalls and thick green wellies on her feet. She stopped a few feet from us and crossed her arms.

"It seems you're not as dumb as most of the people who want something from me."

"Maybe we're just stopping by for a visit," I told her.

She snorted derisively. "Oh please. No one who goes to the trouble of finding my garden does it for the sake of a cup of tea, now do they?" She turned and scowled at Dimitri. "Let Calvin up, for Christ's sake. I believe you've made your point."

Dimitri growled again, but moved off. A moment later he had transformed back into my husband, his face still bleeding from the plant's attack.

"Maybe you'd get more visitors if you didn't sic your enormous man-eating plant on them," he snapped, wiping his cheek. He reached for me and I ran to him. "Lizzie, are you okay?"

"I'm fine," I said with complete honesty. The breastplate had absorbed every one of the plant's attacks, and apart from a little residual queasiness I chalked up to the awful smell, I felt good. "But you're not."

Philippa the Strange rolled her eyes. "The lad's a griffin; he'll be healed up in an hour. But here." She drew a tin out of her pocket and tossed it to me. "This salve'll speed things up."

Dimitri gingerly touched the wound on his head, drawing bloody fingers back. "You expect me to trust anything you give us after your plant tried to kill us?"

"You brought a *dog* into my garden. What did you expect?" she retorted. "Calvin usually knows better than to start things with people, but dogs are a whole other issue. Do you know how much damage a dog could do in here? Besides, Calvin was hungry. He didn't get to munch on the rabbit I lured in here for him because *someone* scared it away."

Dimitri opened his mouth to retort, but I spoke up first. "We do want something." Best to just be honest at this point, I figured. "We need moly. I was told you're one of the few people in the world who has it."

"Moly." Philippa looked to the skies and heaved a sigh. "Always with the moly."

"It's for a spell to save my mother," I continued. "She's possessed, and our coven thinks that with moly we could—"

"Make a spell that drives out the possession, yes, I know of it. I *invented* that spell." She sighed again, but this time it came off more tired than irritated. "The Red Skulls, huh?" she asked, sizing Frieda up and down.

Frieda smoothed her denim shirt dress. "We've changed. We're much less loud and pushy."

Philippa rolled her eyes. "I'll believe it when I see it." She turned away from Frieda. "You—" she pointed a gnarled finger at me "—you come along with me. You two—" she pointed at Dimitri and Frieda "—you wait here with the dog."

"No siree, Bob," Pirate said. "I'm your watchdog, and that means watching you in this creepy-ass garden."

"I'll be all right," I promised him.

After all, there wasn't a scratch on him. Then again, he wasn't going to be happy when I had to go after that spell residue with soap and a fine-tooth comb later.

"Lizzie—" Dimitri began. I got on my tiptoes and kissed him hard before he could say anything else. It was a hot, urgent kiss, fueled by the remnants of our adrenaline and the fact that my very handsome husband was very deliciously naked now.

"I won't be long," I whispered once our lips finally parted. "I have to do this. For my mom."

"Go on, honey." Frieda smiled encouragingly. "I'll look after your boys."

Philippa was already walking away. I ran to catch up with her.

✺ 8 ✺

If I thought I was out of my depth among the herbology in the last garden, there was no word for how lost I felt as we walked deeper into Philippa's domain. Every plant seemed magical. Some glowed red and white, like strings of Christmas lights, while others were shrouded in their own little veils of darkness. We even passed a little patch of pink and white begonias that piped up with "God Save The Queen" as Philippa walked by.

"Those are cute," I commented, more than ready to break the silence.

"*Those* are the result of decades of careful breeding, intensive spellcasting, and more ESL classes than you could shake a stick at," Philippa retorted. "I had to start over completely after that idiot Ant Eater ruined my first crop. *That* put the kibosh on any idea I ever had of joining a coven, let me assure you."

I couldn't picture this woman, who seemed so completely engrossed in her garden, as part of a larger group of witches. Still, the thought that she might have been one of the Red Skulls once upon a time was compelling. "They could have used you."

"Everyone could *use* me, or my plants, rather. But very few people know how to handle my babies, and even fewer can do it *well*." She walked fast for such a short person, stalking past a bunch of murmuring anthuriums, whose volume picked up as she went by. "Troublemakers, those ones," she cast back at me as I passed them. It was strange—like hearing a voice, but having the wind snatch it away at the last minute. "Don't listen to them; they'll drive you batty."

I hustled by, and the whispers stopped. "What do you do with all these plants?" I asked.

"What's it look like? I *grow* them."

"I mean…" How did I say this without offending? "You use them in spells, don't you?"

"Child." Philippa stopped and turned a weary eye on me. "These plants *are* spells in and of themselves. I don't need to chop them into pieces and brew them to within an inch of their lives to find a use for them. They're already useful just by existing."

I was beginning to wonder if I was going to walk away with moly after all. "And you never give them to anyone else?"

"Rarely." She shrugged and kept walking. "Battina was an exception. She knew the value of every part of a plant. I didn't have to worry about her stomping gracelessly through a patch of daisies just because she couldn't slap an immediate use on them." She turned down a smaller darker path, and I had to crouch to get under the flowering vines that made up the makeshift trellis overhead.

"Moly is one of those plants that everyone wants but few people truly know how to use," Philippa said. "It grew out of the blood of a god, you know. The giants were the first children of Gaia, the earth."

Looked like I was getting a mythology lesson in addition to herbology. "I know a little about that but not a lot."

"I figured." She finally stopped and knelt down in front of a low, unassuming-looking crop of little white flowers with slender green stalks. The blossoms looked a bit like tiny bells. "Moly," she said with a wave of her hand. "One of the strongest magical protections known to man. I could sell a single blossom for a hundred thousand dollars to the right taker."

I didn't have that kind of money. Good thing Philippa didn't look like the type who collected boats or cars or expensive purses.

"I'd never sell it, of course," she said, sizing me up. "You refrained from *taking* from me out there, and I appreciate that. It's the only reason I'm still talking to you. Squat." I got down onto the ground next to her. "You need it for your mother, you say?"

I nodded. "We left a doorway open and a demon got into her. Grandma tells me that the Praesidium spell is powerful enough to drive any demon out."

She rubbed a finger along her chin, thinking. "It might be." She spoke slowly, considering the question. "But there's a price associated with moly," she added, pointing the finger at me. "A blood price."

That didn't sound good. "What's a blood price?"

"Moly only grows on ground that's been watered with blood. It has to be transported the same way, or else it seeks out blood to keep itself alive."

Oh my god, what was I going to have to do to get this stuff to Hillary? I stared at the innocuous-looking little plants and tightened my jaw against a wave of nausea.

"Evil acts like a fertilizer," Philippa continued. "That's why you absolutely cannot touch moly. If it gets its roots in you, and you are tainted by the simplest human fault—if you've ever been dishonest, told a white lie"—her eyes bored into mine—"*tried to deceive a garden witch*—well, those moly roots find that deception and feed on it. The roots grow deeper and deeper until the plant consumes you."

Ah, that was why it killed you if you tried to transport it.

"So I definitely can't touch it," I said. I'd done my share of fibbing even before I became a demon slayer. The plant would have me down to bones after ten minutes at one of my mom's Sunday brunches.

Think. My mind spun as I tried to come up with a solution. "Can you put it in a pot?" Or a vault?

Her gaze held mine. "I need blood first."

I nodded.

One of the Three Truths of the demon slayer was *sacrifice yourself.* I had done it before, and for my mother, I would do it again. "How much?"

Philippa peered at me for a long, silent moment then nodded. "A vial should do it."

"All right," I said, even though my mind screamed at me that there had to be a catch. Maybe there wasn't. Maybe this was as straightforward as she made it out to be. It seemed like a small sacrifice, all things considered.

Philippa wore a strange little smile as she reached down into the cargo pocket of her overalls and withdrew a vial and a needle. With a nurse's precision, she readied her instruments.

"Do you want to move to some place more sterile?" I asked, swiping at a few gnats buzzing close by.

Her eyes flared as her gaze shot to me. "We do it now."

She held out a hand and I gave her my arm. Philippa gave no warning as she plunged the needle into my vein. I held still, bracing myself as we watched my blood gurgle into the vial.

"Nice," she said under her breath. "Very nice."

The needle gouged into my skin. And when she'd filled the vial as much as it could possibly allow, she drew the needle out of my arm with a satisfied smirk.

"You're far too happy about this," I said, placing my thumb over the blood seeping from my wound. I supposed it was too much to ask for a Band-Aid.

Philippa capped off the vial of my blood and held it to the light. "This is wonderful," she crooned, "lovely." She turned to me with a smile. "Even better than I imagined," she added as she placed the vial in her breast pocket.

Wait. "Don't you need that blood to give me the moly?"

She laughed. "Slayer blood? It's far too valuable." She patted her breast pocket. "I'm keeping this as payment."

Holy Hades. She'd tricked me. Blood was a valuable spell ingredient. It was life itself. And now she had mine.

"Give it back," I ordered, advancing on her. "Don't force me to take it from you." She might have her crazy plants, but I was still a demon slayer.

She took a step away from me, and I saw the fear in her. "Pay for the moly, or you'll never get it out of this garden." She saw me hesitate and added, "Your mother can't survive without it."

She didn't know that.

But I didn't want to take the risk. I needed that moly, and trick or not, she wanted my blood in exchange.

Grandma was going to kill me when she learned what I did.

"Fine," I gritted out. "Keep the blood. Give me the moly. Now."

She gave a sharp nod. "We'll use the rabbit that started this whole mess in the first place."

She put two fingers in her mouth and whistled—at least, I assumed she whistled. I couldn't hear a thing, but a minute later a familiar brown bunny hopped down the path. It stopped in front of Philippa, nose twitching contentedly.

"You little rascal," she scolded it. "You were supposed to be a nice, hearty meal for my Calvin. Instead you caused a huge mess. Time to pay for that." She picked the rabbit up and held it against her chest with one hand as she reached down and tugged firmly on a single stem of moly with the other. It took a bit of doing, but she finally pulled the plant free from the ground.

Sure enough, the root dripped red. "What have you got buried under there?" I asked, not sure I wanted to know.

Philippa smirked. "Not as much a *what* as a *who*, dearie, and never you mind about that." She gently placed the root on the back of the rabbit's neck, and—

In the blink of an eye, it vanished beneath the fur. The rabbit squirmed for a moment then settled down again, not even seeming aware of the flower that now grew out of the base of its head. "There you go." She patted it on the back then handed it over to me.

I took it. It was soft and warm. "You just killed a bunny."

Philippa appeared surprised for a moment then smiled. "Don't worry. A bunny is incapable of evil. That root will be easy to get out. Gertie will know how to do it."

"Good." At least somebody would come out of this okay. I held the rabbit tight. "If you're lying to me, I'll be back."

She raised a brow. "One lie and you're so untrusting." Philippa studied me for a moment. "Just manage your expectations, Lizzie. Even Odysseus's luck ran out a few times along the way home. Now leave me alone and don't step off the path on your way out."

I backed away, refusing to give her the advantage. When she was well behind me, I turned and hurried back to Dimitri, Pirate, and Frieda with our quivering prize clutched to my chest.

❄ 9 ❄

By the time I got back to the others, the scene of near carnage had completely changed. Dimitri's face was almost totally healed, the wide slash across his cheek diminished to a thin line that probably wouldn't even have time to scab before it was gone. Frieda bent to brush some mulch under a patch of cobra plants and leapt back when the petals reared back and tried to strike. Pirate chased his own tail in an effort to chew on a clump of defensive spell gook.

Calvin, I was pleased to see, stood completely still. Like a regular plant. *That's right, you'd* better *play dead, mister.*

Pirate saw me first. "Lizzie! Can you help me reach my—oh!" His voice changed from plaintive to gleeful in a heartbeat. "You brought back the magic bunny! I was hoping you would." He leaned up onto my leg and sniffed at the rabbit's feet. "Do you think Flappy will like him? He could be Flappy's pet just like Flappy is my pet, and—"

"Oh no," I said, cutting off that line of thought before Pirate could really get going. "We aren't adopting another pet. Two is enough."

"Two?" Pirate quirked his head. "Who's the second one?"

It wasn't worth trying to explain. "Never mind. We're not keeping him. He needs to live free."

Pirate tilted his head. "What if the other bunnies make fun of him for having a flower growing out of his head?"

"A what?" Dimitri joined us. Judging from his ripped pants and black, now sleeveless, button-down, Frieda had apparently managed to spell together enough of Dimitri's clothing that he wouldn't be arrested for indecent exposure the minute we stepped back out into the real world. Thank goodness the van had tinted windows. He looked like a shipwreck victim. "Yeah, I know. These were my favorite pants."

The guy was having a hell of a birthday.

Dimitri looked down at the rabbit, then at me. "Is that the moly?"

"Yeah."

"Another bloodthirsty plant." Dimitri swore in Greek. "Growing *on* the rabbit, or *in* the rabbit?"

"I have no idea." I'd stopped being surprised by what these witches did. "As long as we get back to Grandma soon, he should be fine."

He placed his hand on my bloody arm. "What price did she ask for it?"

"Nothing I wasn't able to give." I'd made plenty of bad deals in my day, but I always got the job done.

"We'll discuss this later," he said through a clenched jaw.

It was already done. "We'd better get out of here," I said. The rabbit started kicking, and I clutched it harder. The *last* thing I needed was for it to get free in the middle of a poison garden, eat something fatal, and drop dead before we could get it home.

I stuck a Sneak spell on the rabbit, and we left the poison garden and its less-than-gracious inhabitants behind.

Getting back out into the Botanical Garden was like stepping through the looking glass and into the real world again. I tilted my head back and sighed with relief as the sun beat down on me. No man-eating plants or cobra orchids. Just a mega-powerful witch who now had my blood.

"Hey!" a throaty voice called.

A man in a security guard's uniform hurried our way, a frown creasing his wide face. "You're not allowed to be on the grass here! And what—is that a *dog*?"

Oh jeez, Pirate had lost his Sneak spell. "He's a service dog," I blurted.

Pirate was chasing his tail in a circle again. The guard looked unconvinced. "He's an emotional support animal," I clarified. "And we were just leaving."

The guard nodded once. "I'll walk you out."

Five minutes later we were back with the van, and I called Grandma to let her know we were on our way.

"You *got* it?"

She didn't have to sound so incredulous. "Yeah, we should be back to the condo in about—"

"Oh, we've moved on from there," she broke in. "The condo couldn't be any more secure at this point, and your mom was getting antsy. We're back at your folks' place. Ant Eater's got her warding teams going, and your dad just put out the buffet. Seems it was too late to cancel the catering for Dimitri's birthday."

"As long as you've got it handled," I told her. I didn't want to take any chances.

"We're set." Grandma whistled. "I swear, Lizzie, I could eat off the bathroom floor, it's so damn clean."

"Just don't try it," I warned.

Hillary had the place professionally cleaned every week. She had for as far back as I could remember. I remembered getting annoyed as a kid to come home from school and find all my toys put away in the wrong places.

"Well, now it's clean *and* warded," Grandma said with satisfaction. "I'll start the prep work on the spell." She paused. "You *sure* you got out of a tangle with Philippa the Strange with no ill effects? You're not bringing any curses home, are you?"

"Pretty sure." I'd bring up the blood when I had time to listen to a lecture. "Philippa doesn't remember Ant Eater kindly, though."

"Nobody holds a grudge like that woman," Grandma grumbled, and ended the call.

"New plan," I said, turning to Dimitri and Frieda. "We're going to my parents' house." The bunny kicked enthusiastically in my arms. "How are we going to keep this little guy contained?"

"I've got an old milk crate in the back of the van," Frieda said. "He should be safe in there."

"Great." I handed him over to her. "It won't take long to get there." My parents lived in a posh Atlanta suburb with a golf course on one side and a series of nature trails on the other. If we took Rock Springs Road, we'd be there in under fifteen minutes. That was good—I felt more run-down than I should have, even after a fight. I was going to need an afternoon nap at some point.

With traffic it took twenty minutes, but eventually we ended up in front of my parents' million-dollar mansion. It was an immense two-story brick house on three acres, with a meticulously maintained lawn, a pool house, and a pavilion in the back for entertaining. After such a long time away, it looked more like Barbie's Dream House than anywhere I would ever be comfortable.

Frieda pulled off her helmet and whistled. "Darn, honey! What's your daddy do again?"

"He's in finance." That was Cliff's standard answer when people asked. It was nicer than saying "he's a stockbroker—yes, like the ones your parents warned you about."

I wasn't really even expecting him to be home, and it was a genuine surprise when he met us at the door.

Cliff was classically handsome, with thick silver hair and a

WHAT TO EXPECT WHEN YOUR DEMON SLAYER IS EXPECTING

friendly demeanor. He wore a polo shirt and chinos—very casual, for him. He must not have gone in to work today.

"Lizzie!" Cliff pulled me into a hug, and I was so stunned, I let him. It was pretty nice. Neither Cliff nor Hillary had been the most demonstrative parents, but at least Hillary had been around. Cliff had spent most of my childhood at work or at work parties or on work trips. Hugs were a rarity. "It's good to see you." He let go of me, turned to my husband, and held out a hand. "Happy birthday, Dimitri. Good to see you too." His eyes flicked over Dimitri's torn clothes. "Is that what the kids are wearing these days?"

"Gardening mishap," Dimitri said smoothly. "I'm fine, though."

"I'm glad to hear it," Dad said, as if he didn't quite believe it. The man had, after all, been through the demon invasion at my wedding.

He opened the door wider as Pirate raced past him. My mom bought the expensive dog food and always left a bowl out when Pirate came to visit.

"Good to see you too, Frieda." Cliff held his elbow out to her. "You're looking especially lovely today."

She smoothed her Gap denim dress. "You should have seen me yesterday," she told him.

"I believe there are some ladies waiting for you in the kitchen," he continued, ignoring the rabbit tucked under her right arm as only a true Southern gentleman could.

"Bless my soul!" Frieda mock-fanned herself before accepting his escort. They headed through the foyer to the kitchen. I followed more slowly with Dimitri and smiled when he wrapped his arm around my shoulders.

"You okay?" he murmured as we walked across the marble floor. Prints of landscapes and golf courses lined the walls, and here and there was a tasteful plinth bearing a vase of my mother's roses. I didn't even know what to call Hillary's sense of decorating style, but it worked for her and Cliff.

77

"I'm fine," I said. "Just a little tired."

"Well, I did keep you up late last night."

"And I woke *you* early this morning." Gosh, was it just this morning that everything had been so much...simpler? Life came at you fast when you were a demon slayer.

"True." He looked like he was going to say more, but just then my mom appeared in the doorway leading to the living room.

"Lizzie?"

She was back in her own version of casual clothes, Ann Taylor slacks and a cream-colored silk blouse, but she still looked kind of off. Weirdly delicate in a way my mother never was.

"I'll go take Pirate out back," Dimitri said, and left me alone with Hillary. I approached her and was immediately pulled into my second hug in under a minute from one of my parents. It was a little *Twilight Zone*, to be honest, but if anyone needed a hug right now, it was my mom.

"It's going to be okay," I assured her. "I got what we needed to complete the spell. Everything is going to work out fine."

"Of course it will," she replied, as confident as ever, but her grip on me didn't let up.

"I'll take care of you," I promised.

"Oh, Lizzie." Finally she pulled back, her eyes a little moist. "That shouldn't be your responsibility. I'm the mother here. *I* should be the one doing the caretaking." She sighed. "I feel bad we had to put off Dimitri's party. Is he upset?"

"Not even close," I said. "And even moms deserve a break sometimes, right?"

Cliff came up behind Hillary and put a hand on her shoulder. "Right," he said firmly. "Come on, darling, have a seat before you wear a hole in the carpet."

"Oh, you," she scolded him, but she did go and sit down on the couch. Cliff put his hands in his pockets and looked at me.

"Demonic possession, huh?"

I winced. It sounded kind of bad when my straight-laced father just out-and-out said it. "Yes. But we're fixing it."

"Don't interrogate her, Cliff," Mom chastised.

"I'm not interrogating anyone," he said mildly. "I just want to know who I have to thank for that getup you had on earlier." He pulled out his phone and turned it on. "It's going to be my new background," he said, showing me a picture of Hillary in all her catsuit glory. "I'm thinking about getting it printed and framed."

"Cliff." My mother rolled her eyes at him, and he smiled impishly in return. It was the most playful I could ever remember them being, and I wondered if it was because of the situation, or if I'd just missed these moments as a kid.

"You found what you needed, then?" Hillary continued. "Were there any problems getting it?"

None that she needed to hear about. "No, it all went pretty smoothly," I lied.

"Oh, good." She did seem to relax a little bit, the fine lines around her eyes smoothing out. It felt surprisingly good to be able to comfort her—like I was dealing with her as an equal rather than child to parent. "I have to say I'm looking forward to getting this *thing* out of me. It's rather uncomfortable."

I sat down next to her. "You can feel it? What's it like?"

She frowned, one hand going to press lightly on her blouse. "It's like...like a hand inside my chest, scraping. Then it curls up like a fist. It feels like it's trying to grow bigger."

Well, *that* was hideous. I was spared having to come up with the appropriate platitude by the arrival of Grandma, who carried a steaming cup of potion on a delicate china saucer. My mom's eyes narrowed.

"Did you get that out of the china hutch in the dining room?"

"Sure did!" Grandma said. "I believe it was you who told me just earlier today that 'presentation is everything.'" She winked. "I figure this stuff might be easier to get down if you drink it from a pretty cup."

Mom didn't look appeased. "You picked a tea set out of my limited edition wedding china from *Lenox*?"

"Didn't look like it sees the sun much, honestly. Why have it if you're not gonna use it?" She passed the saucer over to Hillary, who took it gingerly. "Bottoms up!"

Hillary stared into the cup, which contained a thick reddish brown sludge that was still bubbling around the edges. "Wonderful." She pursed her lips, then brought the cup to her mouth and tossed back the contents like she was chugging from a beer bong at a frat party. I was impressed.

Hillary lowered the cup slowly and set it back on the saucer, her face carefully expressionless. She swallowed hard once, then again.

"Do you want some water to wash it down?" I asked a little anxiously.

"I think—" She raised a hand to her chest again. "I think I—*oh*—"

Oh, no. "Mom?"

Before I could reach out and touch her, she slumped forward, almost falling off the couch until Cliff got his arms around her. Her teacup skittered across the carpet, leaving a blood red stain in its wake.

I turned to Grandma, who watched wide-eyed. "Is this supposed to happen?"

"No," she said, and I felt my heart turn to ice. "The demon should have exited her body as soon as the potion hit her stomach."

"Did she get enough?" I demanded, checking her pulse. It was thready, weak.

"Yes," Grandma insisted. "Yes. One sip was enough."

"It's okay, sweetie," Cliff murmured on repeat, not fooling anybody as Dimitri took her from his arms and carried her gently to the large couch by the window.

"Let me see her," Frieda said, brushing past Dimitri, digging for a diagnostic spell. I knelt by her side as she ran the purple, glowing spell over Mom.

She lay still and pale against the white fabric.

"Well?" Grandma demanded, pushing her way in.

Frieda shook her head. "Blood pressure is low. I'm giving her something to stabilize it." She drew a glittering pink spell out of a pouch and glanced at Cliff, who gave a quick, worried nod as the blonde witch pressed the spell to Mom's throat.

Mom gasped, and I nearly had a heart attack. But then her breathing steadied and some color returned.

"Is she okay?" Pirate asked, jumping up onto the couch. I let him curl up next to her.

Frieda cast a sad look back at me. "That's all I can do."

"But she looks better," I insisted.

Grandma placed a hand on my shoulder. "She's fading fast."

I closed my eyes. "Are you sure?" But I knew. The moly hadn't worked. We were running out of time.

Frieda nodded. "We need to get this thing out of her, Lizzie."

"We will," I promised. I just didn't know how.

꙰ 1 0 ꙰

I was about to ask when the nausea that had been bumping
up against the edges of my consciousness all day suddenly
surged back full force. I clapped a hand over my mouth and
raced to the nearest bathroom, making it to the toilet just in
time to lose what little was in my stomach.

Vaguely I felt hands pulling my hair back, and Grandma's
voice called out, "Frieda, get in here!" I wanted to reassure her,
but I'd have needed to catch my breath for that, and I just
couldn't. I threw up hard enough that my stomach cramped and
my eyes watered, and there was nothing I could do to stop it.

Eventually I calmed down enough to recognize the feel of
Dimitri's arms around me, his lips murmuring against my ear as
he held me up. "Relax, there you go," he whispered, and when I
finally nodded in agreement, I felt him shudder with relief.

"Tell Frieda to stay with Mom." I was fine.

Really.

"Water," Grandma said tersely. She held a cup out, and I
took it with shaking hands, rinsing out my mouth and spitting
before sipping it slowly. I felt like I was in the middle of the

ocean, being tossed from wave to wave. The nausea surged and fell with every crest and trough.

I weaseled my way out of Dimitri's arms and sat down on the blessedly cool, clean tile floor.

"Lizzie." Grandma knelt beside me. "Do you have an allergy I need to know about?"

"No," I whispered, my throat on fire.

"Did you have any reaction to the moly when Philippa gave it to you?"

I shook my head.

"I didn't see anything," Dimitri added.

"Okay." Grandma nodded comfortingly. "Good. Then tell me straight: what did you trade Philippa for the moly? Because I know she'd never give it away for free."

"My blood," I said, and her face fell into furious lines. "Just a vial."

"It doesn't take much to wreak havoc!" Grandma shouted, making my head swim again. "What if she's messing around with your life force right now? Damn it, Lizzie, I thought you knew better than this!"

"I do," I croaked, "but I did what I had to do to save Mom. You'd do the same thing for me."

She didn't bother denying it.

Grandma pushed to her feet with a groan. "Well, we might have been hoodwinked, then. That potion should have worked." She rubbed a hand over her face. "Why didn't it work?"

I didn't have an answer for her. I sat on the bathroom floor with Dimitri for another minute, riding out another wave of nausea. He didn't say anything. He simply held me, but I could feel his anger in the tension of his arms and the grit of his jaw against the top of my head. It was like clinging to a live wire.

In retrospect, I could see that I should never have given my blood to Philippa, but hindsight is twenty-twenty.

At the time, I was sure she'd needed my blood to transport

the moly. Never in a million years did I imagine she'd keep the vial. It had been a miscalculation, sure. One that would cost me.

My head throbbed, but the churning in my stomach began to let up.

It wasn't as if Philippa would have waited to use the blood. Whatever would happen was already set in motion.

One thing was certain: sitting on the bathroom floor wouldn't help.

"I'm okay," I said, pushing back a little against Dimitri's hold.

It would have been a consolation if the big anti-demonic spell had worked, but my mom was worse off than ever. It wasn't like I'd find any solutions in the powder room.

Dimitri didn't release his hold. "You don't feel okay," he said, his voice soft yet bitter. "You just puked your guts out, and you're still shaking like a leaf. You need to be more careful."

"I know that," I snapped, wriggling out of his arms. This time he let me go. "I made a bad choice," I said, staggering to my feet. "I'm allowed to make a mistake." I braced a hand on the immaculate porcelain counter, for emphasis and in order to stay standing.

"You are," he said, standing, "but not many more like that." He paused. "I'm worried about you."

"I get it." I ran a hand down my face, as if that would keep my head from throbbing. "Look, I'm sorry it didn't go right in the garden. I'm sorry the spell isn't working, but I'm not sorry for trying."

I glared at him, and to my surprise, a slow grin crossed his face.

"I'm not sorry, either." He kissed me sweetly on the forehead. "We'll get through this. We handled Philippa last time; we can handle her again if we need to. At least now we know what to expect."

I nodded, but something about the idea didn't sit right with me. "If she's the one who's behind this."

Dimitri leaned a hip against the counter. "The timing is too close to be a coincidence. Why else would you be getting sick right now?"

"I don't know, but we can't assume it's her just because of that. And we can't pin what's happening to Hillary on our encounter with Philippa the Strange." We didn't have *any* concrete ideas when it came to my mom now. The defensive spell to end all others, the one the coven had been so *sure* about, hadn't worked. But why?

I turned toward the mirror. "Give me a few minutes to clean myself up, and then I'll join you out there."

My legs still felt a little watery, and I was sure Dimitri could tell, but he didn't argue.

"Call me if you need me," he said with a gentle brush of his hand against the small of my back.

I nodded as he left, shutting the bathroom door behind him.

I kept a hand on the counter as I opened the medicine cabinet, finding what I'd known would be there on the second shelf—a little travel-sized bottle of mouthwash. My mother's cleaning service stocked every bathroom just the same, whether it was attached to a guest suite or not. I cracked the seal and tipped the bottle into my mouth, swishing viciously, like the burn might be a tiny penance for the fact that I had no idea what to do next.

Hell, *nobody* had any idea what to do next. Not Dimitri, not the witches, and not me. I was just as stumped as—

Wait. Not *nobody*, now that I considered it. Someone had already told me in no uncertain terms that he could help us. I hadn't listened at the time. I'd been so confident that we could fix my mom without resorting to taking his advice. Now, though...

The biker witches would have my head, but that was preferable to watching my mother fade, knowing I still had one thing I hadn't tried.

I wasn't being reckless. I was simply being practical. Even if the thought of speaking to him again made me wince.

The spirit had helped me once before with no ill effects save for his obsession with me. I didn't want his fixation to grow, but my comfort wasn't worth my mom's life.

I stared at my pallid, messy reflection in the mirror and cleared my abused throat roughly. "Hello?"

Heck, I didn't even have a name for him. Or a way to call him. I'd told him to move on and leave me alone.

"Um..." I reached out with my mind. "You...?"

Hello again, Elizabeth.

I bent my head as his voice filled my mind. It was a relief and an invasion at the same time.

There's no need to be nervous, he said smoothly and a little too delightedly. *After all, you called me.*

Naturally, now was the time he was going to be a smart-ass. I stared down at the shell-shaped sink in front of me. "You know what I'm after." I kept my voice low so I wouldn't tip off anyone who walked by.

I do. You want to know how to save your mother.

He said it like a tease. He knew he had what I wanted. Damn him.

He hummed thoughtfully, and I winced at the way the sound seemed to vibrate inside my skull.

I take it your other avenues of exploration have all come to nothing.

I closed my eyes tight. "I wouldn't be asking you otherwise."

*There's no need to be snippy. I'm simply...*grateful *that you're finally acknowledging how useful I can be.*

Yeah, well, I felt less grateful and more desperate, but I was pretty sure that was what had the spirit jacked up in the first place.

I lifted my head to stare at my splotchy red face in the mirror, as if I could see him inside me. "What do you know?"

I know that it isn't surprising that your spells and potions haven't worked.

Okay, that was new. I turned and leaned against the sink. "Tell me why."

I swore I saw the flit of a shadow in the corner to my right.

I saw the creature inside your mother, he said, as if he were unveiling a grand gift for me. *I can see it now,* he added with relish. *It's not a demon.*

"It has to be," I said, my head spinning a bit. "My mom smelled sulfur, and we know Grandma didn't ward properly after Xerxes."

Call it a demon-adjacent, he offered. The shadow in the corner grew darker and began to slink down the wall.

The creature isn't in and of itself a demon, but it's attracted to them.

The shadow drew down to the floor.

It feeds on their magic, he said as the presence slunk toward me. I took a step to the left. *Demons leave traces of energy. It finds those and feeds off that lingering power. Think of it as a demonic scavenger. A long-distance parasite, if you will.*

"Lovely," I said, placing a hand on my switch stars.

The shadow halted its advance.

I might not like this spirit from New Orleans, but I would never have thought to look for a demonic scavenger. "Why haven't I heard of these creatures?" Rachmort had never mentioned them to me, and he worked in purgatory. The spirit had always led me right in the past, but I needed more to go on here.

They're exceedingly rare and exist in a space between dimensions. Hell is for the vast and powerful; Limbo is for the sorrowful and neglected. Scavengers are neither.

"Great," I groused. I had enough trouble with the big baddies, much less new ones. "And halt it," I warned as the shadow began its slow advance once more. No way did I like being indebted to this thing.

The spirit gave a small chuckle, as if this were a game instead of my mom's life we were talking about.

Demonic scavengers live in a tiny sliver of the astral plane called the

Scour, the most barren of all wastelands. Very dreary. Scavengers are the only creatures that can live there for long, and even they would cease to exist without feeding on the energy of others. Dark energy is their first choice, but they'll take advantage of other sources if presented with them.

Like my mom's life force.

"Okay." I pushed off the counter. "If this scavenger has a connection to demonic energy, then why can't I get rid of it?" Demons and their ilk were my specialty, for the love of Pete. They could be hard to kill, for sure, but I had taken out everything from succubi to Hell's own royalty. With any luck, a scavenger would be way easier to handle than either of those.

What good parasite makes it easy to be evicted by its host?

I could ask him the same thing, but I didn't. It would be rude, and I needed his help.

I imagine the scavenger was attracted to the remnants of Xerxes's energy in your home. Your grandmother trapped it with her ward as you fled. It probably latched onto your mother out of desperation. Your witches banished it with their wards yesterday, but didn't see the connection, much less sever it.

The weakness in my knees was back, and this time it had nothing to do with an upset stomach. "So the thing has retreated to the Scour and is still feeding off Mom's life force."

Quite safely, I might add. Unless the link between them is broken, she will continue to fade and eventually die.

This was a nightmare. I sat down heavily on the white toilet cover. "How do you know all of this?" I asked quietly.

I've traveled far and wide in my search for knowledge, Elizabeth. After all, the more you know, the harder you are to defeat. The shadow inched toward me once more. *Let my knowledge keep you from defeat now.* His tone switched from lecturing to cajoling. *All you need from me is the method and a bit of guidance along the way.*

I opened my mouth to answer, but a sudden knock at the door stopped me cold. "Lizzie?" It was Grandma. "You okay in there?"

"I'm good." I reached back and flushed the toilet. "Just finishing up in here."

"Your mom is awake."

Thank God. "I'll be there in a second."

I stood. The nausea was almost gone. I didn't have time to screw around anymore. We needed to attack this thing that had her and get rid of it once and for all.

"What do you want for your help?" I asked the spirit. Philippa's price tag had just bit me in the butt. I at least needed to be clear about what my buddy from New Orleans had in mind for me.

You'll pay me back when the time is right, he oozed.

"And what will you ask?" I pressed.

Nothing you can't give. I would very much like you as a friend, Lizzie.

"A friend, huh?" I scoffed, drawing out a switch star, taking a perverse pleasure when it halted the spirit. "I've seen stranger things," I admitted. "In the meantime, tell me what I need to do."

<hr>

BY THE TIME I EMERGED FROM THE BATHROOM AND GOT BACK TO where Hillary lay on the couch, her head resting on Cliff's lap, everyone was looking at me like they expected me to double over any minute. Dimitri started toward me when I walked in, but I shook my head. I was feeling stronger. Maybe it was the fact that I had a plan.

I knelt next to her. "How are you feeling?"

"Better," she said, forcing a weak smile. "How about you?"

Asked like a mother. "I'm fine," I assured her. "I think I know how to cure you of this."

She grabbed for my hand. Hers felt weak, cold. "I knew you would, honey."

"Well, don't sit on it," Ant Eater piped up from behind us. "Whatcha got?"

"Mom," I said, refusing to talk over her or about her, "I think your life force has been tapped by a scavenger." I gave them the spirit's explanation for the creature, how it worked, and why it had gone after Hillary. "Luckily, getting it out is pretty simple. All I've got to do is follow its trail back to the Scour and bait a trap for it with a little of my own energy. When it comes after me, I kill it. Problem solved, Mom is saved, and we all go home happy."

Only nobody looked happy, not even Cliff and Hillary.

Ant Eater strolled to the side of the couch and stared me down. "Where'd you get all this?" she demanded. "I've never heard of scavengers before, and I've been around the block a few times."

"Oh, I reckon she got it from her spirit friend," Grandma said flatly before I could try to explain. "Didn't you, Lizzie?"

There was no point in denying it. "Yes."

Grandma slapped the window hard enough she could have shattered the glass. "Damn it, kid. What did I tell you about being in its debt? What does that thing want from you for its help?"

"It doesn't want anything," I insisted. "It told me what I need to do to hunt the scavenger down, but that's all. I haven't opened myself or my powers to it, and I'm not planning to, either."

Grandma planted her hands on her broad hips, and her anger was palpable to the point her eyes practically glowed. "Plans don't count for shit when the going gets tough."

She was an intimidating sight. But I refused to be intimidated.

"The going is already tough," I pointed out. "Mom's getting worse."

"It's not bad," Hillary said from where she lay. She tried to sit up for a moment, then eased back down onto the cushion with a faint groan. "It's not particularly pleasant either," she confessed.

We both knew she was fading, but I wasn't going to keep

saying it in front of Mom. "Tell me *your* next step, Grandma, because we don't have time to wait and see anymore."

We stared at each other in silence for a long moment. Eventually Grandma deflated a bit, relaxing her rigid stance with a huff. "How are you supposed to find this scavenger when you can't sense it inside Hillary? How can you track down what you can't even see? A minute ago, you were puking your guts out."

"I need your magic. I need you to open me up to the other realms and then I can bait a trap for this thing."

She stared at me for a second too long.

Frieda leapt to her feet behind Grandma, stumbling over her tennis shoes. "We can do that," she said with relish.

Ant Eater shot her the evil eye.

"There are thousands of unexplored realms," Grandma began, but I could tell she was at least thinking about it.

"We don't have to go in that lost," I told her. "I go in with Mom, and with my power amplified by yours, I should be able to see the thread of the scavenger's hold on her. I follow it back to the Scour, set the trap, and wait for the scavenger to come to me." I patted the switch stars on my utility belt. "Then I kill it."

"Then you kill it." Grandma's lips twisted like she wanted to spit. "Easy peasy, just like that. But nothing is ever that straightforward, Lizzie, especially not when it's being fed to you by a spirit who hasn't even set a price."

Yeah, I didn't like that part, either.

I fixed her with a cool stare. "I'm still waiting on your solution. Give me another choice, or help me with this one."

Ant Eater closed her eyes. "You already owe him just for telling you this."

"In for a penny…" I said to Grandma.

She looked like she could chew nails, and just when I thought she'd explode into a fit of rage, she exhaled in a rush. "Fine," she snapped. "We'll do it. We'll find this Scour and let you trace this predator, but I want veto power over the situation.

We monitor you and Hillary with our own magic, and the second I think you're in over your head, I'm pulling you out of there whether you're done or not."

I was ready to argue, but then Hillary spoke up. "I agree with Gertrude."

I had to admit I was a little shocked. "Mom?"

She started to shake her head then grimaced. "Help me up, Cliff." He got an arm under her shoulders and slowly lifted her into a sitting position, keeping her flush to his side the whole time.

"Lizzie." She sighed. Her eyes were sunken and her skin deathly pale. "I know we haven't always seen eye to eye on a lot of things…"

Ha, that was an understatement. We hadn't seen eye to eye on most things. From the time I graduated college and went to work for a preschool instead of finding a more prestigious job, right up to my wedding when I'd had to fight with her on everything from the guests to the dress, I'd always carried around the knowledge that I was a disappointment to my adoptive parents. It had strained our relationship to the point where even our twice-a-month Sunday lunches had felt like too much at times.

Mom pursed her lips, as if she knew what I was thinking. "Despite my…insistence on some things in your life, I never, ever want to put my welfare ahead of yours." She looked up at me, so full of love that it staggered me. "You're my daughter, and I need you to be as safe as possible. If you got hurt—or worse—trying to save me, I would never recover from it. *Never*." The raw honesty left me speechless. "So no extra risks, all right? Let your friends take care of you the way you're taking care of me." Tears welled in her eyes. "I'm glad you found them."

"Mom—" Now it seemed as if she were saying goodbye. "We're going to get you through this," I promised.

"Just know that it might get messy," Frieda added, as if we'd asked her.

"So no Dior?" Mom teased.

"Not with live frogs," Creely told her.

Grandma scratched the phoenix tattoo on her arm. "We'll need a place that's easy to ward. Not too big."

"Big enough to fit us all. Preferably close to water," Ant Eater said, thinking out loud. "Protection spells love water, and we're going to ward the hell out of this place."

"We need privacy," Frieda added. "The last thing we need is a visit from the neighbors."

"Or the police," Grandma added.

Mom and Dad exchanged a look. "I think I have just the place," he said, stroking her forehead.

She gave a small nod. "Go ahead and escort the ladies, dear."

❧ 11 ❧

D ad led us out toward the pool house. The backyard
looked like a page out of a magazine and reflected my
mom's style, from the colorful white and yellow striped deck
chairs surrounding the pond-shaped swimming area to the thick
white columns of the portico.

The pool house stood about twenty feet away from the main
house, the two buildings connected by a brick walkway with a
cedar-tiled portico overhead.

But by the time I got down to the pool house itself, it was
clear the witches had staked their claim well before we'd decided
to do a ceremony there.

Sidecar Bob had broken out my dad's enormous barbeque
and set it up right outside the sliding glass doors. He sat in front
of it, turning unidentifiable skewers of meat over the fire with
all the care of a master chef. Pirate sat at his feet, offering
helpful observations.

"Be careful, or you'll burn it! And nobody likes burnt
squirrel. Okay, well, I do." Pirate licked his chops. "I like any
kind of squirrel."

"Not the raw kind, Pirate," Bob replied, scooting his wheelchair farther forward, reaching for the skewers in the back.

Ugh. There were those of us who didn't like squirrel either way. At least I was able to handle the smell without gagging.

"This is great." Grandma nudged Cliff as she eyed the small white building behind Bob. "Now do you have a chain saw I can borrow?"

To his credit, Cliff gave a quick nod and set off to find one.

"And so it begins," I said, holding my arms out to Pirate.

"Err…" He scooted closer to Bob. "I've got a thing."

Right. My own dog was too busy working an angle to snuggle with me.

Meanwhile, Grandma stomped past me, calling out instructions to the rest of the coven.

"Dimitri." Ant Eater brushed past me to get to my man. "You're in charge of the altar. We need a slab of wood; anything but pine, the harder, the better."

"I'm on it," he said, planting a quick kiss on my cheek before heading back up toward the house.

Just where did he think he was going?

"What's my job?" I asked Ant Eater.

I expected a snarky answer. Instead, I got a firm clap on the arm. "Save your strength," she urged.

Right. Nice way to remind me that this all came down to me in the Scour.

"Aww…Lizzie." Pirate nosed my leg. "Go ahead and pick me up." I did, snuggling my face into his wiry hair for a moment. One of the biker witches had given him a bath, thank goodness, and now he smelled vaguely like patchouli. There were times a girl just needed her dog. But as soon as it began, the moment was over. Pirate squirmed to face me and planted a wet nose on my cheek. "We're having a squirrel-beque, and I'm the head chef's assistant! How many chunks can I put you down for?"

I wrinkled my nose where he couldn't see it, then pulled back a little to get a look at him. "None for me, thanks. I just ate."

His little tail drooped. "But, Lizzie, Bob and I have been slaving over a hot grill for...for *minutes!* Many minutes! More minutes than I have paws, and that's a lot. You have to try some!"

Um, no. But I didn't want to hurt Pirate's feelings, either. "Sorry, buddy, but no squirrel meat before big magic, that's the rules."

Pirate grumbled for a moment then turned his head toward Sidecar Bob. "Hey, Bob! Is there any possum meat left?"

"Nah, we're fresh out of possum." He glanced at me and winked. "I'm sure Lizzie won't mind if you take her share of the squirrel, though. We don't want it going to waste."

"Yay!" Pirate squirmed until I put him down then ran back over to Bob. "I'm ready for samples!"

Not too many, I mouthed at Bob, who nodded his graying head at me. That done, I headed into the pool house to see if there was anything I could do to help.

The *water* part of the pool house was pretty compact, one of those high-tech endless pools that pushed a current so you could swim forward while basically staying in place. My mom swam up to three miles a day, which was kind of crazy considering she claimed she kept fit by walking from event to event to facilitate being "seen." The water was still for now, the air filled with the scent of chlorine and warm to the point that the glass walls were completely fogged over.

None of the fluorescent overhead lights were on, and with the sun now below the tree line outside, it was actually pretty dark in here. I reached for the light switch.

"Nope!" Grandma batted my hand away before I could make contact. "None of that. I've got people bringing in plenty of candles; those'll do us just fine." Through the gloom, I saw

ANGIE FOX

Creely bent over, taking measurements and marking out spots on the tile floor—with a literal marker; I hoped it wasn't a permanent one.

Ant Eater barged in, leading a group of witches who began hanging bunches of dried plants from the ceiling and over every door and window.

"No time to hunt down fresh herbs. We found these in the van," Grandma said with a head shake. "Good thing we've got plenty of extra stores after New Orleans. That's a prime city for magic—we hardly made a dent in our stash."

New Orleans had been a little *too* good of a city when it came to magic. I remembered the parade of the dead marching down the street, while tourists snapped photos without understanding the horror they were looking at, and I shuddered. "What can I do to help with the setup?"

"Nothing at all." She stepped to the side to allow Frieda in. Frieda had a familiar goat skull in her hands, and she seemed to be whispering to it as she walked by.

I frowned. "I know you want me to save my energy." I'd been a little tired lately. "But if I don't keep moving, I'm going to lose my mind."

"Lizzie, darlin'." Grandma put her hands on my shoulders and looked me straight in the eyes. There was compassion there, but also determination. "Trust me. We've got this. You should be focusing on how you're going to track down this scavenger once we get the ceremony set up. You've never done this before, and we're probably only gonna get one shot at it. Make sure it counts." She gave me a little squeeze then moved off toward the pool.

How could I even begin to plan when I didn't know what I'd be facing?

I headed back outside so I wouldn't crowd the witches, sat down on a lawn chair shadowed by one of Hillary's rosebushes, and did what I dreaded.

I closed my eyes, focused, and addressed the spirit. "Hey," I said, not too thrilled to be having the conversation. "If you're there, let's go over the game plan again."

As you wish, he said, nearly making me jump.

It seemed he was always there.

For you, he said, finishing my thought.

I opened my eyes and saw that I'd fisted my hands to the point that my nails dug into my palms. Slowly, I let go, keeping an eye out for my shadowy friend.

"Don't mess with me," I ordered.

He chuckled. *So hostile,* he said slowly. *So full of life.*

I never should have invited him in.

I'd barely finished the thought when he began:

Once the witches provide the power to push you beyond the veil, I will guide you to the Scour. We will locate the scavenger that has possessed your mother, and we'll set the trap for it.

"How?" I demanded.

Your energy is vastly more suitable for its consumption than hers, and it will be drawn to you like a moth to a flame. Then you shall kill it, and all shall be well.

"How does the trap work, exactly?" I'd asked twice already and still hadn't gotten a clear answer.

The trap is nothing more than a framework for your energy, completely harmless to you but challenging to construct. I can construct and maintain it far more readily than you could hope to, and speed will be important in the Scour. It won't be healthy for you to remain close to it for long.

I had a brief vision of being stranded in outer space, surrounded by nothing but black emptiness—frozen, airless and alone. I blinked and shook my head.

"Don't put pictures in my mind."

You said you wanted to see. I really am helping you.

Perhaps. The spirit wasn't trying to get me killed—of that, I was sure. What he wanted from me after all of his help…well, I'd handle that once my mom was safe.

Your focus should be on providing the necessary energy to bait it then taking care of the scavenger once it's hooked, he continued.

I could handle that. Heck, I'd literally torn my soul in two before in order to kill a demon—this wouldn't be nearly as severe. "What about—" I paused as I watched three of the biker witches carry an enormous flowerpot that had just recently held a bunch of geraniums toward the pool house.

A mottled tentacle emerged from the pot, covered in greenish slime and writhing maliciously. Before I could even pull a switch star, one of the witches reached out and slapped at it with a skinny bundle of tightly woven twigs. The tentacle cringed and pulled itself back into the pot.

"Don't even think about it!" she snapped, and they all walked on. Typical day with the biker witches.

How very eldritch, the spirit commented approvingly. *Your coven is pulling out all the stops.*

"Why would they need anything sinister?" I balked. "We're not going to Hell."

Better to have the proper tools on hand than to be caught wanting.

Look who was a Boy Scout all of a sudden.

I was distracted from my helpful spirit by the sight of Dimitri appearing around the side of the house, carrying a massive wooden rectangle over his head. He'd changed out of the torn clothing he'd worn out of Philippa's garden and I couldn't help but admire how his biceps strained his T-shirt to the breaking point. His expression was pretty serene, though. I wouldn't even have known he was feeling it if not for the faint shine of sweat across his brow and along his neck.

Hillary had told me once that women didn't sweat, they glowed. Dimitri was living proof that sometimes, men glowed too. I got up and walked over to meet him. "Need any help with that, hot stuff?"

He winked and lowered the wooden slab to the ground next to him. "I think I can handle it from here."

I looked over the wood with interest. "Wow, this is great," I marveled. The last time the witches had done a ceremony like this, they'd cobbled together several different pieces of redwood to make a big enough altar. This thing could have doubled as a life raft on the *Titanic*. "Where did you find it?"

Dimitri scratched his chin a bit sheepishly. "Did you know there's an empty house a few blocks down?"

My jaw dropped. "Wait, did you…" Now that I looked more closely, I could definitely see *hinges* on one side of the enormous piece of wood.

"I don't think it's a door that anyone will miss. As soon as the ceremony is over, I'll take it back."

"It might be covered in tentacle slime by then," I warned.

Dimitri raised an eyebrow. "Do you know anything I don't about this ceremony?"

Ugh. "Never mind. I'm sure it'll rinse off."

"Aha!" Grandma walked up next to us and ran her hands over the door. "Black walnut, excellent choice. Black walnut for the altar will be like injecting nitrox into your astral projection, Lizzie. Boomer! Jude!" Two witches broke off from the hubbub around the pool house and came over. "Let's get this inside and sigiled up." She turned back to me. "Five more minutes and we should be good to go. You might want to grab Hillary."

My guts clenched. "Right." I hated seeing my mom fade away, but I had to keep it together now. Just a little while longer, and this would all be over. I'd save her.

I had to.

Dimitri kissed the side of my head. I turned and our lips met. No one was better at revving me up or soothing me to calmness than Dimitri. "I'll go with you," he said once we separated. "I can help carry her if she needs it."

Turned out, she needed it. She didn't *want* to need it, brushing off our attempts at first, but when Hillary almost fell after getting to her feet, Dimitri made an executive decision and just swept her into his arms.

"Oh my." She blinked up at him then looked archly at Cliff. "Are you taking notes, dear?"

"Of course." He winked at her, but the moment Dimitri turned away, he took my hand with a worried look. "Lizzie…is this thing you're doing safe?"

"Safer than letting her stay the way she is," I said with complete honesty. "I have to get the scavenger out of her, or she'll die. With the coven's help, I'm confident I can do this, Dad."

He held my gaze for another minute then squeezed my hand. "You've become a hell of a strong lady, sweetheart. I'm proud of you."

His words touched me more than I could ever tell him. I gave Cliff a quick hug then dashed after Dimitri and my mom.

The witches had been doing this for longer than I'd been alive. We could pull this off.

The alternative was unthinkable.

Dimitri, Mom and I entered the pool house side by side, which was good, because if I'd been in front, they would have run into me when I stopped abruptly.

The place had been completely transformed. All the windows were covered with cloth, creating a cave-like atmosphere. The smell of sage hung heavy in the air, the primary ingredient for the Red Skulls' wards. I guess they really didn't want the scavenger following me back from the Scour and manifesting here. Good thinking.

The only light came from thick red candles melted in place on the tiles, creating the shape of a pentacle. A biker witch sat behind each one, chanting in unison with each other—but completely silently. I could sense the movement of the air in and out of their mouths, but I couldn't hear anything. Each of their chins was painted with a black squiggle that looked familiar, but I'd definitely never seen a spell before that literally enforced silence.

Grandma sat cross-legged about a foot back from the black

walnut door, which now had a pentacle burned into the wood. I winced internally. Maybe we could sand it out before we put it back? She waved us over. A brass gong was set up on her left, the goat skull on her right. In the center of the altar was a familiar-looking bunny rabbit on a leash, chewing contentedly on a bundle of herbs.

"Aw, really?" I asked before I could help it. Using animals in rituals like this was a safety precaution, like having a canary in a coal mine. The bad energy you might encounter, demonic or otherwise, would take them out before it got to you, giving you time to save yourself. I'd used guppies and even birds before, but never a creature as big as a rabbit. Especially not one that had escaped near-death already today.

"Safety first," Grandma said primly. *She* wasn't wearing one of the squiggles, I noticed. "You and Hillary get up on the altar," she continued. "Once you're ready, tell me, and we'll start charging things up. And be careful, Lizzie," she added. "Hell is one thing, but strange dimensions no one else has ever heard of require special handling."

I nodded firmly. "I've got it." Dimitri laid Hillary down gently—she was either asleep or unconscious now—and I positioned myself so that I was cross-legged by her head. He backed off to the edge of the room to watch and wait—Dimitri would be the first to admit he didn't know anything about witchcraft.

"Ready?" Grandma asked me.

I nodded. "Ready."

The water of the pool in front of us was totally black now, shivering slightly as a dark form swam beneath its surface. Grandma murmured an incantation, and the light from all the candles flared.

This was it. Now or never. I had the power of the witches. I had the love of my parents and the backing of my husband. I could do this.

I closed my eyes.

"Are you there?" I asked the spirit.

Ready and waiting, Elizabeth.

He sounded different now. He wasn't just in my head but beside me, above me, all around me. I could almost feel his essence covering every inch of my skin, and I suppressed a shudder. "Back off," I warned him.

The psychic pressure relaxed. *My apologies. I'm simply learning the shape of your energy so that the trap I construct fits perfectly.*

"Well, do it from a distance."

Oh, I think I have what I need now, he purred. *Look down into the water. I believe that will be the simplest way for you to share my vision.*

I looked. For a few moments I saw nothing but depthless black before a coal-red spark appeared in the center of the pool. It darted like a firefly on speed, leaving a crimson trail that gradually took on a familiar shape. With a start, I realized that the spark was painting a picture of me.

It looked like a statue done in wire—lovely, but hollow.

The spark vanished, leaving behind the me-shaped trap. I stood alone, as alone as I felt, against the murky black.

Now reach into your core, the very seat of your vital energy, the spirit murmured. Once again he felt too close, like his lips were hovering just over my ear. *Slice a bit of it free and send it into the trap. I will anchor it there and guide us both to the Scour.*

The meditation-speak he was using on me was a little confusing, but I understood what he meant. I focused on the power inside me, on my demon-slayer strength and the way it infused every corner of me. That energy was like a roaring flame, and I only needed a candle's worth to bait the trap. I separated a tiny bit of energy and visualized it settling into the wire frame, expanding and filling it.

Goooood, the spirit hissed. *Perfect. Now, to set the bait. Tread carefully.*

All of a sudden, the image changed from the trap to a swirling nexus, almost like a portal, but this was different, darker.

There was no light on the other side of that, I knew. It felt like being pulled toward a black hole. The larger it loomed in my vision, the more uncomfortable I became, as though my skin were crawling with ants. Even though I couldn't see anything through there, I could feel a dark presence just out of reach. Unconsciously, I whimpered.

Be easy, the spirit said. *The trap is laid. We will wait just beyond the darkness. Once the scavenger is seduced and has begun to feed, I will close the trap. Are you with me?* he pressed.

"I am," I whispered.

As you pull your energy back to you, the scavenger will be forced to come along. Patience. You'll grow more accustomed to the feeling soon.

Patience, *ha.* He didn't even have skin to crawl or hair to stand on end. Moments later, the image of the trap faded.

It has gone into the Scour.

I nodded, feeling the tether of my own energy connecting me to it. I focused on that tether, feeling it bend and stretch at the end of my line.

My stomach hollowed as a darkness crept up on the edges of the trap. I could feel it in my bones and fought the urge to run like hell.

The wickedness lapped against the edges of my power, tasting.

Not yet, the spirit murmured. It spoke from the center of my forehead, like it was using my own third eye to see. The skin there began to itch. *Not yet...*

The scavenger became bolder. I could feel it, testing icy teeth on the base of the trap.

Wait...

Slowly, it began to climb, leaving nothing but a lifeless chill in its wake. It scaled the red energy frame, the feet, the knees.

It reached mid-thigh.

I felt my own thighs go numb.

A little more...

The chill enveloped the trap's waist.

Now, Elizabeth! the spirit snapped. *Pull it back!*

I heaved my energy. I dragged the darkness and the trap with all my strength and will and power back through the nexus, back through the dark beyond.

The water began to bubble and froth.

I let out a cry as I pulled harder.

I could see it!

The glow was dulled, its brilliance banked by distance and dimensions and the scavenger's formless bulk. I felt its insatiable hunger, its unyielding lust for power and strength.

It wanted me.

I heard Hillary groan like she was waking up from a long sleep.

Yes! I pulled harder.

"Her eyes are open!" Ant Eater hollered.

My breath came in pants, my power stretched. I grinned and reached for a switch star. It was time to finish this.

"Now!" Grandma struck the gong as hard as she could.

All of a sudden I could hear the witches again, shouting a familiar chant as the black squiggles on their chins manifested into Ant Eater's winged spell from New Orleans.

"Darkness, danger, black as night, be ye blocked by witches' light! Coven strong and power bright, keep thee out of mine own sight!"

The scavenger arched its back and howled. I almost lost my grip!

"Calm down!" I shouted at the witches. "I'm trying to get a good shot!"

The room was shaking. The trap listed from side to side. Out of the corner of my eye, I saw the witches' spells split into millions of tiny golden specks. They filled the pool house, lighting it up like Vegas.

"Stop it!" I ordered.

They flew in a monstrous wave of light directly at my head.

I took my shot anyway. It went way wide right before the spells slammed into me.

"Aaah!" I shrieked and flung up my arms, but they impacted me like hundreds of warm feathers. The spells covered me with protective energy, blocking out everything else.

I lost my hold on the tether. The scavenger dropped away with a furious howl, and the spirit vanished.

I lost him! I couldn't believe I lost him.

I scrambled to the edge of the pool, brushing away the witches' feathery magic, trying to see past the blazing light and magic remnants floating down and the spots in my eyes from the sudden switch from dark to light.

"What did you do?" I demanded, scanning the swirling depths of the pool. The water had lightened back to green. I could see the bottom. It was awful.

"I had it!" In my grip. "You made me lose it!"

The witches had never blown a trap like that, not that we'd ever done a trap, but they'd never screwed up a mission before. I turned and saw Grandma glaring at me, her arms crossed, ready for a fight.

It was as if she'd done it on purpose. "What the hell did you do?" I demanded.

"I saved your life," Grandma shot back, "probably your afterlife as well."

Fat chance. I shot to my feet and strode to her. "I had the scavenger right in my sights! I was about to smash it!"

Grandma met me halfway. "It didn't look right. It didn't smell right. Hell, it didn't act *right.*"

And suddenly she was the expert? "It's a scavenger from the Scour. How's it supposed to act?" It was dark and creepy. Stinky, too. What else did she want? This was ridiculous. "You'd never even heard of one until the spirit told you about it."

Her expression darkened. "Told *you,*" she countered. "And I don't know what that was in the pool, but it wasn't a creature of the dark. If it was, our wards would have gone crazy." She pointed at the bags hanging over every window. "They didn't even twitch. There was no new evil coming into play, Lizzie. The only evil we're dealing with is the one *you* invited in."

Okay, that was the reason for the silence spells, for the covered pots of who-knew-what, and for the witches refusing to let me help set up. They were shutting me out. They didn't trust me!

Unbelievable. "You haven't been with me from the start." Apprehension flashed over Grandma's face, but she didn't deny it. She'd gone in to this thing convinced we were taking too much of a risk. And then she'd made it a self-fulfilling prophecy.

She dug her thumbs under her belt. "That spirit is bad news, Lizzie."

"I know that." I wasn't an idiot. Although it seemed I'd been a fool to trust the biker witches—my friends, my own grandmother. I ran a hand over my face. This was a disaster. "Look, I get that I shouldn't be messing with the spirit. That part's a no-brainer," I admitted, expecting my New Orleans buddy to pipe in and defend himself.

I glanced around the room when I didn't detect any sign of him.

"We warded him out," she said. "He can't touch in here."

"Banished by light magic," I mused. I wasn't surprised. More annoyed. I planted a hand on my hip. "It seems you've thought of everything," I concluded. "Except how to save my mom."

Grandma sighed and glanced to Ant Eater, who shook her head. "Yeah, we don't know that," she admitted. "But I swear he was playing you. We all saw it."

The witches behind Ant Eater nodded.

They were against me. Every damned one of them.

That was when I saw Dimitri, my Dimitri, standing behind them. It about broke my heart. "What do you think?" I said, by way of warning.

"Lizzie…" His shoulders stiffened. "It didn't look good from here. I think we need to be smart."

"Smart," I repeated. "Safe and completely ineffective," I ground out. I couldn't believe I was looking at the Red Skulls. "Screwing me as I had a grip on the scavenger," I added, addressing the room. "Risking my mom. That's smart." My own husband. My grandmother. My friends. They were never with me from the start.

I spun in a circle. "Damn it!" We blew it. "You could have told me before I dragged that thing out of the Scour. Before I risked my life and my mom's."

Hillary lay next to the pool, still as a ghost.

The sight of her helpless and forgotten made me want to scream.

I went to her and got down on the floor next to her to see how she was doing. Her breath came shallow, and her eyes fluttered open. "Baby?" Her voice was barely audible. "Did it work?"

No. No, it *didn't* work, because my friends didn't trust me. Because they were too scared to pull the trigger. Heck, even the *bunny* looked unfazed, still calmly nibbling on herbs at the far side of the altar.

My mom's utter trust, my friends' utter failure fractured something inside me.

After all this time, all the work I'd done to prove myself

worthy of being a demon slayer—the *last* demon slayer, the one everybody depended on—and all the efforts I'd made to show the Red Skulls that I was worthy, they'd gone behind my back. They hadn't had enough faith in me to work with me, despite my connection to the spirit. They hadn't believed I was capable of taking care of myself and defeating the scavenger that had my mom.

Now my mother was paying for it.

I locked eyes with Grandma. "Get the spirit back."

"Oh no," Grandma said firmly. "We banished that creep outside the wards, and that's where he's staying until we get to the bottom of this."

"There isn't time for that!" I stood between Mom and the coven. "*She* doesn't have time for that! Look at her. She isn't getting any better. Shouldn't she be getting better if I'm being strung along?"

"We haven't worked out all the connections yet." Ant Eater said, frustrated. "That doesn't mean we're wrong."

Maybe not, but it did mean my mom could die while they were piecing their stupid puzzle together. I had felt the darkness of the scavenger, though. It had been true evil, raw and intense. That was more real than any of their hunches. I wasn't going to sacrifice Hillary on the altar of the coven's suspicions. Not when I could still save her.

I needed to get the spirit back.

I reached for a switch star. Grandma saw me and her eyes went wide. "Lizzie, don't—"

Too late. I fired it straight at one of the dangling wards over the nearest window, sage and white yarrow and who knew what else entwined around a protective crystal. My switch star cut through the satchel like butter, shattering the crystal before swinging back to me.

"Lizzie! What the hell?" Ant Eater demanded.

It wasn't enough damage to affect the entire ward, just providing—a blip. A brief moment of openness. That was all the spirit needed to surge back inside the pool house and into my head.

Elizabeth! Oh boy, he sounded pissed. *I'm stunned at your betrayal.*

"Join the club," I told him. "I had nothing to do with that spell."

I felt his anger, his white-hot rage.

I turned my back on Dimitri and the witches. I needed to get to work. "Tell me what's happening to my mother."

Fools, all of you, he fumed. *That spell interrupted the removal of the scavenger at a crucial point! It knows you're after it now and will be ten times harder to hunt and destroy.*

"Why am I not surprised?" I said under my breath.

It is consuming your mother's life force at an accelerated rate in its haste to flee.

I fought back a curse and turned back to the group. "It says the scavenger is still attached to my mom," I announced. "I'm going back in after it. You can help me, but if you betray me again, I'll never forgive you."

"Damn it, Lizzie." Grandma flung her arms out. "You weren't watching, but the rest of us saw the wards tremble harder the deeper you got. The evil was getting stronger. It was getting stronger because it was transferring its hold to *you.*"

Little did she know, I didn't feel very strong at that moment. The queasy feeling from earlier had surged back full force, bringing with it a light-headedness made worse by the fact that I was *sharing* my head right now.

We had to get this done. Now. My mom was running out of time. In fact—

"Mom?" A second ago her eyes had been open. Now they were closed. Her skin had taken on the waxy appearance of someone who had been lying in bed for too long, sallow and tight to the bone. Her mouth drooped open, but no sound came out. I couldn't even tell if she was still breathing. "Mom?" I got on my knees and knelt down close to her, pressing my ear to her chest. Oh no, oh no, oh please…

"Let me in, honey." Frieda pushed through, her usually cheery face unnaturally grim. She pressed two fingers to Hillary's neck while sprinkling a glittering white powder over her face and chest. After a moment, the powder went from white to yellow then started fading into brown.

Frieda shook her head. "I hate to say it, but you might be right. I'm so sorry." The brown powder crumbled to ash. "She's still alive, but her spirit is almost gone. It's being eaten up." She looked at me mournfully.

She reached into her cleavage and pulled out a plastic baggie with a single oily-looking leaf inside. "I grabbed this off one of the plants in Philippa's garden," she confessed to me as she opened the bag. "Devil's Parade, really rare stuff. One little scratch with it can jump-start the heart. It's dangerous, but if we don't revive Hillary enough for more diagnostics, we won't know the best way to help her."

I am the best way, the spirit whispered in my ear. *I am the only way you have left.*

I knew it was a bargain with a baddie. No pure and noble spirit hung out in the Scour and took notes on scavengers. No white presence would invade my mind like he did.

I watched Frieda pry my mom's jaw a little farther apart, then very gently brush the leaf across her tongue. Hillary swallowed reflexively; then her body jackknifed as she lurched into a sitting position and started coughing.

"Uh-oh, too much?" Frieda looked somewhere between proud and concerned. "I've never actually used this stuff before, but it's got a real powerful rep."

I wrapped my arms around my mom from behind and helped lower her back down to the wooden surface of the altar. "Mom?" The witches stood a short distance away, conferring with each other, tossing spell suggestions around and arguing over methods. It didn't look good.

WHAT TO EXPECT WHEN YOUR DEMON SLAYER IS EXPECTING

"How do you feel?" I asked my mom.

Hillary cracked a weak smile. "Like I just got dug up out of my own grave, to be honest."

Nope, no graves. None of that. "We're going to fix it," I promised her. "We've still got time, Mom. The first try didn't work—" *because someone was playing me, and it's hard to know who* "—but I'm not giving up. I'm going to save you."

"Oh, honey." She reached up and clumsily patted my cheek. Her fingers were as cold as ice. "I think...I think it might be time to just let me go."

"Not in a million years," I promised.

"Lizzie." My mom's eyes filled with tears, which dripped down her cheeks and vanished into her lank hair. "I heard... some of what they were saying. Not all, but...enough. This is too dangerous for you."

I was already shaking my head, but Hillary wouldn't be silenced. "It is, and I don't want that. That's the last thing I ever wanted. You just...have to let me go, honey. I'll be fine."

"You won't be *fine!*" Part of me wanted to scream, another part wanted to curl up on the floor and cry. I saw the evil creature that had a hold on her, and I worried for her very soul if she were to pass away right now. "You need to stay with us," I told her.

This was about more than life and death. Worse, it was my fault. That stupid condo—I should have bit the bullet and faced my past long before now. I should have made sure it was clean and safe instead of ignoring it and my mother.

"Oh, baby." She smiled at me again, but it was little more than a tremulous quirk of her lips. "My baby...I know I didn't give birth to you, but I waited so long, and I wanted you so badly." Her eyes closed, and I had a feeling that if I didn't do something fast, they would never open again.

This wasn't right. She deserved better than this.

It's now or never, Elizabeth. The spirit's voice wound around me like a silk scarf, clinging and tightening uncomfortably. *We still have the framework of the trap. Fill it again. But not just a sliver of power this time. I'm sorry, but we need more now to tempt a wary scavenger. You have to give it everything you've got.*

I nodded, wondering if it was even possible. Everything I had? I was exhausted. I felt so sick my arms trembled. My flesh felt feverish, and a metallic taste brewed in the back of my mouth. None of that mattered, though. I was a demon slayer and I had a job to do.

I took a deep breath, closed my eyes and reached for my power. It burned hot and ready for me.

I could do this.

Instead of isolating a section of it and teasing it away from myself this time, I went for the sledgehammer option. Messy and fast, I broke down the barriers between my magic and my mind.

Good, Lizzie. Good…

"Just be ready with the trap." We had one shot.

I knelt before the pool, next to my mother. I watched as the waters darkened and began to swirl.

Yes.

There, as the waters churned, I saw the red outline of the trap.

That's it. Slowly now. Bait it.

I opened the connection all the way. I poured my powers, my life force, my *being* into it, lighting it up strong and bright. The witches behind me gasped.

This is it, the perfect bait.

The scavenger wouldn't be able to resist it. I had it now.

A dark presence shot through the water, like a shark after prey, straight for my energy. Just a few seconds more!

Yes! The spirit lurched inside my mind.

The trap snapped shut. The open bars closed into a solid wall of red.

Damn it. "Too soon," I shouted as the scavenger made a hard dive.

The power of the spirit surged. I felt it surrounding me, suffusing me. Invading me.

I fell forward, and this time it was Hillary who caught me. Her hands felt icy cold, and when I managed to raise my head and look at her, I saw bone-deep fatigue. But she was up, and she was alive.

The dust that Frieda had sprinkled on her was sparkling white.

I looked back to the churning water, now fading to dark green, to lighter.

"Not again," I protested, gripping her, swallowing against the tightness in my chest and head.

"Oh god," Hillary moaned, panic breaking out in her voice. "I'm so sorry, Lizzie!"

I was too, for her, for me. I didn't want to live without my mom.

Then I felt it, the trap was inside me! It pulsed smugly, taunting me, clutching my powers tight and not letting a hint of them through.

Grandma stood over us. "Damn it. What's happening?"

"The spirit," I whispered, barely able to force the words past my lips. "It's—locked them away. My powers." My slayer heritage, my life force, my everything. Everything that made me who I was, that gave me vitality and purpose—gone. The flame had died. I felt so cold.

"I *told* you!" Ant Eater shouted. Frieda slapped her upside the head. Ant Eater continued regardless. "I said that thing couldn't be trusted! Scavenger, my *ass*."

"You're right," Hillary said. She was holding me but not looking at me, her gaze fixed on the fathomless black water of the pool. "There is no scavenger. There never was." She shook her head slightly. "I see it now. It didn't bother hiding anything from me when it went for you."

Her eyes finally met mine, and the pain I saw there was so brutal I almost forgot about my own. "The spirit has been waiting for the right moment to take what he wants, Lizzie. I was the perfect way in for him, the weak link." She sounded disgusted with herself. "He calls himself a helper, but the only person he's helping is himself. He's ready to take what he wants."

"What is that?" I whispered. "My powers?"

"No." She shook her head. "He wants my grandbabies."

❦ 13 ❦

"I'm pregnant?!" I fell back and landed on my butt. *Pregnant.* Of course it had always been a possibility. Dimitri and I hadn't exactly used birth control. But…

Dimitri's back had gone rigid, his eyes wide as he stared from Hillary to me.

"I'm going to have a baby," I told him. I had a psycho spirit inside me…and a baby.

"Babies?" Dimitri asked on an exhale, rushing for me. "She said 'grandbabies.' Does that mean two?" He reached me and bent down. "Here, let's get you off the floor."

I wasn't a weakling. I could stand. Still, I allowed him to help me.

Mom stood as well and gave me a shaky smile. "I'm sorry to shock you, sweetheart, but there's no mistaking what I saw. You're pregnant with twins, Lizzie."

Ha, no. No, there had to be a mistake. Mom's vision wasn't exactly a Clearblue Easy test. "I think I'd know if I was pregnant." I looked to Grandma, who had one hand pressed to her cheek like a startled Southern belle. "Tell me I'm right."

She cleared her throat. "It's not always obvious your first

time around. It surprised the hell out of me too, back in the day, but the symptoms are there."

"General demon-slayer kick-assery?" I asked. It wasn't like I led a normal life.

"The nausea." Dimitri slid an arm around my waist, hand coiling lightly across my midsection. He sounded…awed. "Getting sick really fast and then feeling better the same way. Trouble with foods. Bob said you passed on his barbeque."

"It was squirrel," I informed him.

"Tenderness across your chest," he added, as if I hadn't said anything at all.

Okay, my breasts had felt a little sore lately, but that was residual pain from our big battle down in New Orleans. And my appetite had been off, sure, but we'd been on the road. And…and…

I put my hand over his. "I'm pregnant," I murmured. And as soon as I spoke it out loud, I knew it, *believed* it. "Oh my god."

"You're going to be a great mom," he whispered in my ear.

"To *twins!*" I said, still trying to absorb it all.

His breath huffed against my ear as he grinned. "Yeah."

At the worst possible time. I closed my eyes and wished I'd never gone to New Orleans. That I'd never met that spirit in the upstairs room. That I'd never been a slayer.

Then another terrible thought hit me.

I turned to Grandma. "I'm not supposed to have twins. The count is off. Demon slayer twins are born every three generations." My birth mom was a twin. She shirked her duty and passed the powers down to me. It ended up killing her sister, my aunt. I was the accidental demon slayer. My daughters should get a pass. Then again, the line was messed up now. I just didn't know what to expect.

Only the spirit clearly had expectations. He'd seen the children and sensed their power.

Grandma's expression told me she'd been thinking the same thing. "We'll see what happens."

"Great." Twins, possible slayers, and a spirit who had my power locked in a vault.

And how was I even supposed to manage being a demon slayer and a mom at the same time? Was I going to be able to take on the next big baddie and still take a break to nurse? Babies want to eat when babies want to eat. And did purgatory even have wide enough paths for a double stroller? I supposed I could let the biker witches babysit. The babies would have two dozen crazy aunts with questionable caregiver skills. I could just see my list of instructions: do not let the baby play with live spells; do not give the baby hot sauce; the baby shall not nap in the sidecar of any motorcycle, even if the vehicle is parked.

And what if my babies did grow up to have demon-slayer powers? I'd nurture them, of course. I'd teach them and support them in a way I never was. But oh my god, I'd be really scared for them, too. If they were brash and bold... They'd have to be in order to survive. But it only took one wrong move to be demon fodder. I'd worry every second.

That must be how my mom felt all the time.

I'd never truly considered that before.

Grandma made a motion, and two witches sprang forward to repair the ward I'd slashed. But she was just being cautious. The spirit had already invaded me.

I was the one possessed now, and he wanted—

I reached out and took my mother's hand. "This vision you had. You said he wanted my babies." It was hard to even say the words, more difficult to imagine how I'd protect them. "What exactly did you see? How do you know for sure it's after the twins?"

Tears welled in her tired eyes. "It was all the spirit could think about after the trap closed. He didn't even try to hide it. Everything, right from the beginning, has been because it saw you were pregnant. There was no scavenger. That was a trick to get you to open up. It was all the spirit."

I dropped her hands.

"I'm sorry," she cried. "This is my fault."

"It's not," I told her. "It was mine. I never should have accepted his help in the first place." I'd created the opening. I'd made it possible.

I had saved my mom, and I didn't regret that, but I'd put my life—and worse, my *babies'* lives—at risk in the process.

I closed my eyes and felt the trap inside me, like a weight in my chest, a splinter that had worked its way in instead of out, pressing against my heart and lungs and bone with every tiny movement.

He was inside me, yet he remained silent.

He had what he wanted, and he was biding his time.

I looked to Grandma, to the witches I'd crudely dismissed not an hour ago. The biker witches always had my back. They'd never failed me. In fact, they'd taught me everything I knew. "You guys have always been there to protect me, and I didn't trust you," I said. "I'm sorry. There's no excuse."

Grandma nodded her acceptance.

Frieda shook her head sadly. "You were worried about your mamma."

Ant Eater waved me off. "I don't do emotional bullshit."

"Tough," I told her. It needed to be said. Then came the hard part. "What do I do now?"

I was completely cut off from my powers. Heck, I'd probably cut *myself* right now if I reached for a switch star.

Behind it lurked the malevolent, silent smugness of the spirit. He'd seized my power. He'd wanted my heart. My babies.

"You can't have them," I muttered furiously. "I won't let you."

It's my price, he said, as if it were logical, as if he'd already won.

"I never agreed to it," I raged. "I will never agree."

With all due respect, you have nothing to fight me with. But I like you, Elizabeth, and therefore I will give you a choice.

I stood with my hands on my hips, waiting, dreading as he

played his game. "Spill it," I ordered. I was sick of his manipulation.

Watch your tone, he warned. *Here's the deal: either I take your powers and leave you to die, or I take your children and* their *powers.*

"You're a monster," I gritted out.

I'm a survivor. Just like you. His calm tone angered me, but his next words chilled me to the core. *And, Elizabeth, I was just kidding about you having a choice. I want the babies.*

❧ 14 ❧

"We'll think of something," Dimitri swore to me. The witches had been stunned into silence after I delivered the spirit's message.

"We'll figure this out," I said to him, although I feared in my heart of hearts that we were already beaten. This thing knew my every move.

How could we mount an attack, much less a surprise attack, on a spirit that could literally hear my thoughts?

Ant Eater coughed and glanced to Grandma. "These are all bust now," she said, waving a hand at the ward bags, "but I'm thinking we have supplies for a ward like the one we used to outrun the Banshee of Tulsa."

A bald witch behind her nodded hard. "*Only* one," she warned. "We're out of fairy cross stones, and those damn things take weeks to absorb the spells properly." She glanced at me, apologetic, as if she had anything to be sorry for. "Still, one should last you for a while. Long enough for us to come up with a plan."

There is no plan you can make that I cannot break, the spirit whispered in my head. *No force you can muster that I cannot overcome.*

You can't touch me without your powers, Elizabeth. You are weak now and will grow ever weaker. Give me what I want, and I'll let you live. Deny me, and I will make your last hours on this plane a misery.

"No, you psycho." Not when he wanted my babies. I glanced to the bald witch. "Not you," I added. I turned my focus back to Ant Eater. "Let's do it."

Outside the door, I could hear Pirate shouting, "Lizzie! Lizzie, what happened? Bob and me and your dad all want to know! Lizzie!"

Oh no, Cliff. Of course he was out there, probably worried out of his mind over Hillary. "You should go talk to Dad," I told her. "Let him know you're okay."

She looked at me as if all were lost. For all I knew, it was. "And what do I tell him about you?"

"Tell him the truth. That we're working on a plan to save me…and the babies."

"The babies." Her eyes filled with tears, but she managed a smile. "Oh my goodness, I can hardly believe it. My baby is having her own babies. And *twins!*" I could tell she wanted to gush, but with things so uncertain, she just couldn't quite bring herself to. I appreciated the restraint.

Hillary kissed me on the forehead. "I'll let him know what's going on." She left, and Pirate slipped through the door and jumped up onto the altar.

"Lizzie!" he said accusingly. "You've been playing with Mr. Nibbles without me!"

I could only assume Mr. Nibbles was the rabbit, and was suddenly extremely grateful it had survived the ritual. "We've been working, not playing."

Pirate huffed and licked my chin. "You should have asked *me* to help you. I'm better at work than bunny rabbits. Mr. Nibbles would run at the first hint of danger, poof! Whereas I'm *extremely* ferocious."

I chuckled. It wasn't much, but it made me feel a lot lighter. "Yes, very ferocious."

"I am! I've fought imps and skeletons and, and *dandelions*, because those make you sneeze." He looked at me proudly. "See? I remember these things."

I scratched behind his ears. Pirate panted with joy. "My hero."

"That's me."

I tried to enjoy my dog, the newfound feel of pregnancy, motherhood—I still didn't know what to think about it. Both were better focuses than the witches, who had Dimitri hauling out a garden shovel and other tools to cobble together the new ward.

He was an alpha male and a team player, a man who did what he had to do to take care of the people he loved.

A man who would do anything to save his children.

I sighed. Dimitri would do anything for me, would fight any fight, would fly to the ends of the earth if he had to, but I didn't see how he could help me with this. Not when I was already in so deep.

Please let it be all right.

Thankfully, it didn't take long for the witches to cobble together another ward, this one wrapped tight with a soft cotton cord that ended in a sliding loop. Grandma held the bag in both hands and solemnly delivered it to me. "Give me your hand."

It won't help you, the spirit snarled, shoving against my chest, tearing at my insides as I extended my arm. *I am in you. I have you. The more you fight me, the sweeter it will be when I—*

The bag settled tightly around my wrist, and his voice went silent.

"Holy moly," I whispered.

"Yeah, we used the last of it in there," Grandma agreed.

"Not that," I said. I took a deep breath then sighed it out with a sense of pure relief. "I can't hear him anymore."

Grandma nodded firmly. "Good." She looked me over with a critical eye. "I think the best thing you can do for yourself right now is to get some rest. The Skulls and I can keep at it—"

"All night, if we need to," Creely added. "I've got two cases of Red Bull cooling in Cliff's golf bag." I gave her a double take, and she shrugged. "It's insulated. And I took out the clubs."

"I'll leave you to it," I told her, and them.

It hurt to say. It was like being told I couldn't help prepare the ceremony we'd just gone through, only at least now I understood. The witches had made the right call. And now, it wasn't just that the spirit could overhear—it was the fact that I had no powers *at all*. I was also bone-tired and pregnant. My head ached, and my bra felt about two sizes too small.

Dimitri kept his arm around me as we walked out of the pool house into the warm Georgia night air. Pirate trotted along next to us, but he got sidetracked at the back door to the house, where Hillary met him with a bowl of steak tips.

"I'll watch him tonight," she promised me. "I set up your old room for you."

"Thanks." I nodded.

Cliff stood a few feet away, his hands in his pockets but a deep crease marring his forehead. He watched me with a seriousness I wasn't used to seeing from him.

Our relationship had never been as fraught as the one I had with Hillary, but it hadn't been as close either. He'd traveled in and out of my life as a kid, providing generic approval and gentle affection, but no real memorable moments.

"Are you doing okay, Lizzie?" he asked.

I was happy I could answer honestly. "I'm fine." *For now.*

"For now," he said, which kind of surprised me. "But it's a touchy situation, if what I understand from your mother is correct."

"It is, but…" I shrugged a little helplessly. "Grandma and the Red Skulls are working on it. Right now, I just need to sleep."

"Of course." He opened his arms, and I stepped in for a

hug. "Congratulations, sweetie," he said softly, and I had to fight off a sudden bout of tears. He knew about the pregnancy.

"Thank you," I managed. I wanted to be happy, but I couldn't quite manage it. I pulled back. "I—Dimitri and I are going to…" I pointed at the stairs.

"Okay, Lizzie. Get a good rest."

We walked up the stairs together, Dimitri never taking his arm from me. We walked past four bedrooms because, well, that was my parents' place. But finally, *finally* we reached my old room at the end of the hall, overlooking the backyard.

We walked inside and I shut the door behind us.

The room was just as pink as I remembered—pale pink carpet, a white bedspread with cherry blossoms unfolding across it, bouquets of roses on every papered wall, and a vanity mirror in a pink ceramic frame. Not for the first time, I wanted to open the window and toss it all out onto the back lawn.

But like it or not, this room was part of who I was, part of what had made me into the person I was.

And as I made my way to the glaringly frilly bed, I felt a strange sort of comfort at being back in my childhood room. I didn't belong in this place anymore, but I still *knew* it. It hadn't changed, even when everything else around me did.

My mom had stacked fresh towels on the dresser by the en suite bath, along with two thick, comfy-looking robes. At least my mom had gotten over her "no sleeping together under my roof" nonsense. I walked over to the bed and fell down onto my back. "Ugh."

Dimitri sat down beside me and ran his fingers through my hair. "Do you want to go straight to sleep or shower first?"

Sleep was tempting, but… "Shower," I decided. I was redolent with sweat, tacky with dried pool water and dusted with twelve kinds of spell gunk. I needed to be clean. I rubbed a hand idly over his thigh as I looked up at the ceiling. The ward bag attached to my wrist bumped against both of us. "I'll have to be careful washing. I don't want to get this thing wet."

"Lizzie." There was a *yearning* in Dimitri's voice. I glanced up at him, and he looked solemnly down at me. "Let me take care of it for you."

I tilted my head. "You want to shower with me?"

The corner of his mouth tilted into a sly grin. "Yeah."

That was fine—we showered together a lot, and they usually didn't end up being entirely cleanliness oriented—but there was more at work here. "What's wrong?" *What isn't?*

Dimitri cracked a half smile, but it looked forced. "I haven't been much help to you lately."

Wait a second, no. I struggled to sit up. "Are you kidding me? In Philippa's garden—"

He shook his head. "I'm pretty sure she wouldn't have let Calvin kill us. And apart from that, it's just been you and the witches and this spirit, and with everything we know now…" His free hand bunched into a fist. "I feel useless," he confided, whispering it like a shameful secret. "Like I can't protect you. I *couldn't* protect you, look at you, and I couldn't protect our babies either, and now—"

"You didn't know," I interjected. "Dimitri, you didn't know. Heck, *I* didn't even know things could go this bad. I wouldn't have gotten in this deep if I'd had any idea I was pregnant." That was my own shame to bear.

I felt my breath catch, but now wasn't the time for tears. Fricking hormones. I was so tired that if I started crying, I'd never make it into the shower. "C'mon, let's go clean up. You're in charge."

He took a deep breath, then gently kissed my mouth and stood up. "I like the sound of that."

The en suite bathroom was as pink as the rest of the place, the colors of coral and sand. It reminded me of the beach, which made me pine for our condo back in California. The room was also meticulously clean and stocked with soap, shampoo and conditioner. It didn't take long for the water to warm up—this house had dual hot water heaters. The bathroom became steamy, the mirror fogging over completely, but instead of jumping in, I let Dimitri undress me, piece by piece.

He unzipped my booties and slipped them off, unbuttoned my flowered dress and found the soft lacy bra underneath. My breasts felt achy and swollen, and it was a relief to finally set them free. I closed my eyes and cupped them with both hands, holding them gently, and wondered how I hadn't realized it earlier. I was pregnant, not getting over a massive adrenaline hangover. *Pregnant. Babies. Oh my god,* twins.

Dimitri gently guided me into the shower before I had a chance to freak out. He joined me, keeping my warded wrist by the shower curtain and blocking the spray with his body. He was naked—how had I missed him getting undressed? The man didn't hesitate when he saw something he wanted.

I looked at him appreciatively now, taking in every familiar angle and curve. Dimitri clothed was a sight to see—naked, he put Michelangelo's *David* to shame.

Water hit his back and ran over his broad shoulders and chest in tempting rivulets. The muscles of his arms stood out as he bracketed me protectively, and the dark curls at his groin weren't doing much to hide the fact that he was becoming aroused. Heck, so was I just by looking at him. "Dimitri…"

He stopped me with a kiss—not a hard, demanding one, not a kiss that challenged me, but one intense and worshipful. He caressed me with desperate gentleness, and I melted against him. "Dimitri, *please.*"

He cleared his throat. "Not in here," he said. "We have to keep the ward dry." Unable to tear his eyes from me, he fumbled for the shampoo, finally finding it. "Bend your head forward. I've got you."

I bent, and he wet my hair then lathered in the shampoo. It smelled like orange blossoms, fresh and clean and slightly sweet. I inhaled deeply and let myself relax, surrendering to my husband's tender care.

He washed my hair, then my body, lingering over the still-flat expanse of my stomach and handling my breasts so delicately I barely felt the washcloth. I *definitely* felt his lips follow it, though. My eyes flashed open as Dimitri's tongue laved my nipple, coaxing it into a peak. I gasped and pressed closer to him, barely remembering not to grab his shoulders and pull him in closer. "Dimitri, I need—you." I savored his touch. "Always you."

He pulled away, and his expression was almost feral. "Bed," he said, his voice gravelly with desire. He shut the water off, and we got out of the shower, not bothering to use the towels. He picked me up in his arms, carried me out to the bed, and laid me down. Then he knelt between my legs and—

"Dimitri!" I was already wet for him, and when he touched his tongue to my clit and pressed his fingers inside me, I felt the sharp tug of an orgasm. It would be a fast one—I was so ready for him, ready to come.

He thrust with his hand as he licked me, chasing the taste of me, and I savored every bit of it. Feeling, reaching, needing, I arched my back and wailed, quivering with the force of my own pleasure.

I rocked against him, needing the release he gave like I needed my next breath.

I rode it with him until the tremors began to fade, until I once again felt my back against the bed, my tingling body. I let out a moan. "Oh my god, you're amazing." I made a *gimme* motion with my hands. "Come up here. I want you." I could see how ready he was, his thick cock so hard.

Dimitri smiled, dark and devilish. I shivered with delight.

"Let's try something different," he said.

Before I knew it, he had swept me up and switched places with me, him on his back, me straddling his upper thighs. The head of his cock brushed my clit, and I bit my lip at the sweet zing of pleasure it sent pulsing through me.

"This way I can look at you," he said, and the hunger in his voice made me shiver. "I want to see all of you. I want to watch you come undone for me."

"I always come undone for you," I gasped. It was true. Dimitri brought out my passionate side in a way I'd never experienced with anyone else. I couldn't even imagine my world without him anymore.

If he felt the same, then no wonder he wanted to see me right now. He needed to see that I was here, that I was with him. He needed to *feel* it.

I could do that, with pleasure. I slid forward until the head of his cock was positioned at my entrance, then slowly, carefully I took him inside. Once I finally settled down on his hips, I grinned with pure satisfaction.

Dimitri's eyes were glazed with lust, but he didn't thrust. Instead, he waited for me.

The shower had been about letting him take the lead—but it was *my* turn to take control. I swear the man knew what I needed better than I did sometimes.

And so I took control. I relished the feeling of knowing what I wanted and how to get it. I let go of my pain and my doubt and rode him exactly how I wanted: slow. Slow enough to make him groan. I took and I gave and I cherished him. Us. Before I finally had mercy and sped up.

I braced my hands on his chest as I moved, and his fingertips rose to brush my breasts. He began to thrust, pumping his hips to my rhythm, and I moaned with delight as we rocked together. It was so good. It was always so good with him. I felt filled in every possible way, connected to him more deeply than I used to be able to imagine. He was mine, and I was his, and together we were something beautiful.

Dimitri rubbed his thumbs over my nipples then tugged them ever so gently, and that was enough to set me off again. I ground down against him, every muscle inside me squeezing tight, and this time Dimitri came with me, erupting inside me with a hoarse shout.

I clenched and quivered through the aftershocks until my arms almost collapsed. I settled down against him, and he held me tightly, his face pressed to the top of my head, his arms stronger than any armor.

"I love you so much, Lizzie." He whispered it like a confession, one of his hands coming to rest on my belly again. "I love everything we are together, everything we've made. I won't lose you." The *I can't* beneath his words came through loud and clear.

"I love you too," I told him, pressing a kiss to his collarbone. "We're going to figure this out, Dimitri. I know it."

We would. Or we'd die trying.

❧ 15 ❧

A knock startled me out of a surprisingly deep sleep.

"Lizzie?" my dad's voice called from the hallway. Sunlight streamed through the window right above the bed, searing my corneas as I blinked awake. Ugh, I'd forgotten to pull the blinds. That window had been the bane of my teenage years. I didn't feel much better rested now than I had then, either.

Last night, despite my fatigue, I'd lain awake in Dimitri's arms for hours, my mind running in circles. It seemed like no matter where I turned, there was only more uncertainty. I didn't know how long the ward around my wrist would last, but every minute that passed without a plan was a minute closer to the spirit taking control again.

I couldn't let that happen. Not to me, not to my babies. But I didn't know what we could do to stop it. Even if we found more ingredients for another ward, that wasn't a long-term strategy. The spirit was clever—he would find a way around it eventually. And when he did...

"Lizzie? Dimitri? Are you two up yet?"

Dimitri stirred with a faint groan. I stroked a hand over his shoulder and called out, "Awake but not up, Dad."

"Well, get a move on, honey. There's someone downstairs who might be able to help you."

"Are you serious?" I sat up so fast my head spun. "Who? Is Rachmort back from purgatory?" He never came home early. But maybe this time he did. Maybe he'd sensed something wrong with me and come running.

"Come downstairs and find out," Cliff said, refusing to give anything away. "Your mom left your bags outside the door. There's breakfast down there too, in case you're hungry."

Now that he mentioned it, I was *starving*. My stomach grumbled loudly, and Dimitri cracked an eye and gazed up at me with a grin. "Don't look so surprised. You're eating for three now."

"I am *not*." I boofed him with a feather pillow. "I'm eating for one with two teeny, tiny passengers." I scooted out of bed. "Besides, I'm always hungry first thing in the morning." I'd tried to do sunrise yoga a few times with a few of the other ladies in our subdivision back home in Southern California, but putting off my breakfast for an extra hour meant a stomach so loud it was like having Pirate there with me, rumbling all the way through Downward Dog pose.

Speaking of Pirate, I wondered where he'd spent the night. Probably with Bob, eating leftover squirrel.

Our black leather luggage looked out of place on Hillary's champagne-colored carpet. I pulled both bags inside and cracked mine open to grab fresh clothes.

Clean underwear, new miniskirt, a different bustier…I paused, letting my fingers linger over a heather-purple one. Maybe I'd go with something a little roomier today.

Dimitri came up behind me and rubbed my shoulders. "You could borrow one of my shirts."

"I *swim* in your shirts, babe."

I grabbed a fitted black *Kiss My Asphalt* T-shirt that Grandma had given me for my last birthday, snatched up my toiletries, and headed for the bathroom.

I didn't linger. I couldn't wait to meet Cliff's mysterious helper. It had better be Rachmort.

Please let it be Rachmort. My mentor knew more about demons, spirits, and other big baddies than anyone else I'd ever met.

I hurried down to the living room and stopped short when I saw who sat on my mother's tufted ivory couch. "You have got to be *fucking* kidding me."

"Language, Lizzie," Mom chided from where she poured champagne for mimosas into dozens of crystal glasses on the table.

Language, my ass! I looked around for something to throw. Maybe one of those empty bottles...

"Lizzie." Xavier, fallen angel and deadbeat dad extraordinaire, stood up from the couch with a big smile on his face. A cheap suit hung awkwardly over his frame, and his face appeared even thinner than usual. He'd let his limp black hair grow and had pulled it back into a ponytail. "It's wonderful to see you again! How about a hug?"

"A *hug*?" How about a slug to the jaw? I glared at him so hard he took a step back. It didn't hurt that I had an enormous, glowering griffin backing me up. "Are you serious? After what happened last time, you think you can just show up here and start from scratch?" I whirled on Cliff. "*This* is who you got to help me? Do you know what he's done?"

Hell, what *hadn't* dear old Dad tried to get away with? Since I'd met my biological father, who happened to be a fallen angel —emphasis on the *fallen*— I'd been conned into nearly killing myself to save his soul, offered up as a sacrifice to the Earl of Hell, and worst of all, lied to about how much he wanted to be a part of my life.

I'd never forget the way he walked out on me after I'd risked everything to save him.

Some people just aren't cut out to be parents, he'd told me. Yes, well, then they shouldn't lie about it and pretend just to get what they wanted before walking out.

"What do you want this time?" I demanded.

He spread his hands out in front of him. "I just want to help you, baby."

"I don't need more of your games," I told him flatly.

Killing demons was my calling, but having my heart toyed with like that…it had almost broken me the first time. The second time around I'd thought I was prepared for his treachery, but it had still hurt. When he'd left without a word after I killed his demonic master, I'd thought that was the end of it. I'd let him go and moved on.

I wasn't about to deal with it a third time.

And where did he get off acting like everything was fine? Son of a bitch.

"I can get rid of him right now," Dimitri said dryly, moving from behind me.

Cliff stepped in. "Hold on a second," he said, lifting a hand. "I don't know all the details," he conceded. "I do know that it's all hands on deck here. Your grandmother and her coven are doing their best, but we can't afford to leave any stone unturned." He looked a lot sterner than I was used to. "Just hear him out. After all, I did go to the trouble of bailing him out to get him here."

"Bailing him out?" I glared at my bio dad. "You were in jail?"

Xavier winced, and even that looked slimy. "It was a little misunderstanding, at best. I was *this* close to talking my way out of—"

Cliff cut right through the bullshit. "He got picked up in Reno for cheating at the tables. He also owes a significant amount of money to some pretty…unsavory people."

Xavier did look rather the worse for wear. He was a tall man, and handsome if you liked them lanky, but he'd gone from thin the last time I saw him to practically cadaverous now, and his hair looked greasy.

This was not the man who had played preacher and brought hundreds of congregants to their knees with the strength of his charisma. This was a man who had lost all his charms and was hanging onto life by the seat of his pants.

My heart panged a little in sympathy, but I stifled it. Xavier didn't deserve that kind of consideration. "How did you find him?"

Cliff tucked his hands into his pockets. "I have financial alerts set up for his name, as well as numerous aliases. When he gets into trouble, I find out about it."

I should have been surprised, but I wasn't. I knew Cliff. "You've always been thorough."

He shrugged. "It's not hard to put two and two together. Everything leaves a money trail, and his ruined church left a big one." He glanced back at Xavier. "Following the money can lead to a lot of information."

Oh my god. My biological dad was a screwy charlatan who'd gotten himself arrested, and my adopted dad was a financial tech wizard who'd bailed him out. What was my life?

"What makes you think he'll be able to help?" I asked.

"Lizzie, honey." Cliff cocked his head and strolled over to me. "I know you don't like to involve your mother and me in the demon-slayer side of things. I know it's dangerous and you're trying to protect us, and for the most part I appreciate that. But you're up against something big and bad. And if there's one thing I've learned over the years, it's that when you want to see the inside of a sewer, you find a rat."

"I'll let that pass," Xavier commented.

We ignored him.

"He's right," Xavier tried again. "I can help. I would have come anyway, though," he insisted. "Knowing that you were in trouble—that your unborn children were at risk—that was all the reason I needed to come here."

Dimitri snorted. "You're full of shit."

Xavier laid a hand against his heart, looking wounded. "It's true! I've made plenty of mistakes in my life. I own that, but I'm not so heartless that I would abandon my only child when she needs me."

It sounded good, except...he'd done that. That was *precisely* what he'd done, and not only had I almost died last time, Dimitri had been the one to save me. Xavier hadn't helped keep my family together then—he'd practically destroyed it.

My lips were numb, I was pressing them hard together to keep from screaming at my father. I forced myself to relax enough to speak. "What did Cliff offer you to come here?"

"Lizzie—" he said, too cloying, too practiced.

My head thrummed and my jaw ached. "Tell me. What. He offered you."

Xavier opened his mouth then closed it again. Cliff said it for him. "I paid his bond." The two men exchanged a look. "And his gambling debts."

"Only out of necessity," Xavier insisted. "I wanted to help you as soon as I heard, but how could I do that rotting in jail? And the debt to the bookies had to be paid in order to keep me alive long enough to get here. Here's a secret: when those people say 'your money or your life,' they aren't kidding." He laughed weakly. "So it's not that I'm being paid to be here, kiddo. I *want* to be here."

"You were paid," Dimitri snapped. "I'm with Lizzie. This is ridiculous."

Dimitri was right. I could only imagine how much money Cliff had laid down to get my worthless father here.

"Unless you can come up with something really, really good," Dimitri added.

Wait. "What?"

Mom swept in with another tray of drinks. I wanted to sigh, or shout, or scream. This wasn't an entertaining situation.

Xavier kept his eyes on my big bad griffin. "I was briefed."

"By who?" I demanded.

Mom stopped dead in her tracks. "By Gertrude, sweetheart." At the look on my face, she grabbed a mimosa flute and took a long swig. "She and several of her people already had...*words* with your father. We asked them to do it outside so they wouldn't wake you. By the end of it, she said if she had to stare at his face a moment longer, she'd do something she regretted, so she opted not to join in for this part."

"That's not exactly what she said, Hil." Cliff winced.

My mom sniffed. "I'm not repeating those words. Good grief, she turned the air *blue* with her swearing." She looked at me and said, "*Literally* blue, Lizzie. I didn't even know that was a spell you folks could do."

"I didn't either," I told her.

Xavier seemed to sense an opening. "If I wasn't able to offer any help, I'd already be gone."

"That's the first thing you've said that I believe," I told him.

His expression dropped, but he didn't deny it. He took a step closer to me, then another. "You know your grandmother wouldn't have any qualms about kicking me out if I was useless. But I know what needs to happen next, Lizzie. I know what you need to do to defeat this spirit."

I clutched the ward bag dangling from my wrist. It was still working—I was still alone in my head, but I knew the clock was ticking. I still felt that splinter deep inside my chest, keeping my powers from me. Silence didn't change that.

"What do you think I need to do?" I asked. I wasn't too proud to deny help if he could actually offer any.

His shoulders relaxed a little. "You're going to have to travel between worlds to find the realm where the spirit is residing," he said, as if it were as easy as a trip to the market. "Gertrude told me about the stunt with the scavenger. It's closer to the truth than you'd think, only with the spirit itself as the target this time. Once you're there, you need to sever the ties between yourself and the spirit."

Oh, sure. That was all. "The trick is, I don't have access to my powers. I can't protect myself. I can't even sever anything."

It was ridiculous. I'd never had to deal with this before.

Xavier smiled knowingly. "Powers work differently in the spirit realm. It's a place of…" He closed his eyes for a moment, looking briefly rapturous. "*Endless* possibility." He wore an expectant expression. "You might not be able to access your slayer abilities here, but the spirit realm is a place that deals in echoes. That's all most spirits are, really—echoes of a person's mortality. If you can summon up the feeling of using your powers, then you'll get results."

"No kidding." I shared a glance with Dimitri. It made sense.

"You won't be as strong as you'd be if your powers were still intact," my bio dad added. "But you'll have surprise on your side. That will help."

I took a flute off my mom's tray then set it back down. "Why will they be surprised?"

Xavier took a flute of his own. "Because you can't get there without both me and the witches." He took a swig and wiped his mouth with the back of his hand. "Your spirit is in you. He knows we don't talk. That you hate me. But he can't see us right now." His mouth tipped into a small calculating grin. "Any part I play in this will come as a complete surprise to him."

True.

It was tempting, I had to admit. Taking the fight to the spirit could give me the advantage I needed. But there was still one big lingering question. "What do I need from you?"

His gaze locked with mine. "I'm going to have to guide you there myself."

Oh no. H-E double hockey sticks times two, no.

I reached for a drink again. Mom handed me a regular

orange juice. "You think I'm going to trust you to lead me into a crazy spirit realm?" My dad really was nuts.

"No one else in your group knows how to get there," he countered. "The spirit realm is easy to access from this plane, but the act of transporting yourself there is another mess altogether." He met Dimitri's wilting stare and redirected his focus to me. "It's like the difference between looking at a labyrinth from above versus being down in the middle of one. Without a guide, you won't make it there, and without me to act as a tether back to this realm, you probably won't make it back."

"That sounds like a threat," Dimitri said flatly. I could see his fingers twitch, like he wished he had his dagger handy.

"No threat." Xavier held up his hands, like he were being arrested. Again. "I have nothing to gain from a double-cross. If we do this, my body will be left here along with Lizzie's during the ritual. If I fail to bring her back, I'll be surrounded by witches when I wake up." He arched one eyebrow. "You think they'd just shake my hand and let me off with a 'well, you tried'?"

He had a point. Still, the thought of trusting him made my skin crawl. My father had never, not once, come through for me when I needed him. And now the stakes were higher than ever.

"You don't have to do this," Dimitri urged me softly. "There has to be another way."

"Let me know when you come up with one," Xavier said, too cocky for my taste. "In the meantime I'll be grabbing a snack, waiting for you to come to your senses."

My mom had put out a tray of mini quiches, and Xavier began downing them.

God, he was *infuriating*. Unfortunately, that didn't make him wrong. "And you already talked to Grandma?" I asked sharply.

"I did," he said, not even bothering to turn around. "You can ask her yourself."

"She should have Mind Wiped him," Dimitri muttered.

"But she didn't." Xavier turned around, his hands full of

quiche. "She didn't tell me to leave, either." His eyes seemed to soften slightly. "She knows I'm your best chance."

I felt pulled in too many directions. I needed to think, to weigh my options. I needed a moment to myself, at least mentally. I didn't want to look like I was backing down either.

My mom, the ultimate hostess, provided me with a respite. "I've got to plate a few dozen sandwiches in the kitchen," she announced brightly. "Lizzie, come and help me. You can grab breakfast while you're in there, too."

"Thanks. I think I'll do that." I squeezed Dimitri's hand then turned and followed my mom into the kitchen.

❦ 16 ❦

The fridge was full of food, all of it plated, wrapped and loaded into the stainless steel doublewide like an 'ultimate hostess' version of Tetris. Hillary pulled out platters of premade sandwiches, cheese and crackers, shrimp cocktails and veggies with a half-dozen different types of dip.

"Martha Stewart, eat your heart out," I said, gazing around her immense, tasteful white and gray kitchen as she handed me a platter and went back in for another.

"This was going to be for Dimitri's party," she said as we carried both trays to her massive kitchen island. "But it's come in handy anyway," she confided. "Your biker witch friends really like to eat."

"You don't know the half of it," I told her, refraining from giving too many details. She didn't need details about Bob's penchant for barbequed wildlife.

Too bad that wasn't my only problem. "About Dad," I began, "and my other...dad—" I felt a sudden wave of light-headedness.

"Here, honey, sit." She led me to the reclaimed oak kitchen table, and a chair was behind me before I could stiffen my knees to keep standing. "Take a breath," she instructed. "You came in here to calm down, so let's do that. Then we can tackle the problem logically."

"I am logical," I countered. I prided myself on my ability to plan, to think. "You don't understand what I've had to deal with from that man."

"I know enough," she said, reaching into the cabinet for a plate. "I'm also aware that you have great instincts...when you're not too emotional to use them."

She placed a china plate on the table next to me. It held an oven-warm frittata and a buttermilk biscuit. She topped it off with a cup of coffee made just the way I liked it.

As if food were the solution.

"The coffee is decaf," Hillary said, like she was confiding a sin. "But I figure that's probably for the best right now, and lord knows if I kept regular in the house, your father would *never* get to sleep at night."

"Thanks." If—*when*—everything went according to plan, I would have to start thinking about that kind of thing. Alcohol, caffeine...and wasn't there something about pregnant women and fish? Damn. No shrimp cocktail for me.

"Lizzie?" she prodded, as if I were a disobedient child.

"I'm eating," I told her. I grabbed a fork and took a reluctant bite of the frittata. Flavor exploded across my tongue —tart sun-dried tomatoes, artichoke hearts, feta cheese, spinach and just the right amount of salt. If I didn't know better, I'd think my mom had magical powers, too.

Hillary quirked her lips. "I'm glad I got it right."

On more than one count. "This does taste great. And it *is* making me feel better," I admitted.

She sat down next to me, cup of coffee in hand. "I know Xavier wasn't the best parent."

"He almost got me killed, damned, and skewered by an angry mob," I said, going for another bite of frittata.

Mom took an extra-long sip of coffee. "I don't like him

either," she admitted. "But I was on the other line with your father when he called Xavier. I do think Xavier wants to help."

I rolled my eyes.

"Parents don't always get it right," she said, with a shake of her head. "I've been thinking very hard lately about all the ways I could have been a better mother. I could definitely have been less judgmental, I see that."

I paused with my fork in the air. "You and I are different, and that's given us trouble. It's natural. *Normal*, even. But Xavier? He's a fallen angel with a busted moral compass and no loyalty to anybody but himself."

She nodded thoughtfully. "I think he wants to change." I huffed and she persisted. "I'm good at reading people. You know that. My take is that Xavier is a weak person. He can be a bad person, but he wants to change."

"You're serious," I said, suddenly losing my appetite. I pushed my plate away. "And what happens if he fails in this grand attempt at change and it kills me and my babies?"

Mom's eyes glassed with tears. "I don't know," she admitted. "I just don't know."

I reached out and took her hand. "I apologize," I told her. "I shouldn't have said that."

She squeezed. "It's the truth. I don't want to shy away from that." She pursed her lips. "It's just that your grandmother trusts him—" she gave a small shrug "—or at the very least feels like she can use him." She gazed intently at her hand in mine. "I trust your grandmother." Her eyes found mine. "What else is there to do? We have to have faith, Lizzie."

"I do," I promised. "In you and Dad. In Dimitri." In my friends. "Just not Xavier."

Ant Eater burst into the kitchen from the backyard with Creely in tow. "Lizzie!"

"We're talking," I said quickly.

She hesitated, as if she wanted to keep going. "Ah." Her eyes fell on the trays of food.

"Take them," Mom offered. "I was about to set up a picnic out by the pool."

"I'll get it going," Ant Eater said with relish, scooping up a tray and letting Creely grab the other one.

The door banged closed behind them. "Your grandma has already gotten the witches started on a cave in the backyard."

"A Cave of Visions?" Grandma was serious.

"That's it," she said, as if she had any idea what they were about to do to her backyard. "They really love you," she said simply. "Dad and I do, too." She smiled. "I just hope that, from here on out, you'll count Cliff and I as a part of that group, because—because we really would do anything for you. And I will personally punch Xavier in the face if he even thinks about betraying you or any one of those witches out there."

"I don't think that will be necessary, Mom." Although she did take a lot of kickboxing classes. For all I knew, she could have a pretty good left hook.

I sighed. Mom had been a lot of things to me over the years, including some bad things, but now more than ever, I was realizing that for all our differences, she had never failed to come through for me.

"I take that back," I told her. "Feel free to punch Xavier whether he messes up or not."

She smiled.

"And you were wrong before," I told her. "You've been a wonderful mother to me." My birth mother had foisted off her responsibilities on me and abandoned me. Hillary had always wanted me, then and now. "I just hope I'm as good to your grandbabies as you've been to me."

Mom burst into tears and hugged me. I held her tight and felt every bit of her love.

"I'd do anything for you," she murmured against my hair. "Anything. Even welcome Xavier into my house."

I drew back. "Let's get him out of here as soon as we can."

"We will," she said, wiping her tears and patting her hair.

She nudged my plate. "Eat up," she said, standing. "I've got to get this food out to the ladies before they start hunting down the local fauna."

Maybe Mom knew more than she'd let on.

I ate, probably faster than I should have, but I was *hungry*, darn it.

Now that I'd decided to go with Xavier's plan, now that I'd be going into the spirit realm tethered to my deadbeat dad, I needed all the strength I could get.

I finished the frittata, demolished the biscuit, and was sucking down the last of the coffee just as Hillary came back inside. "Oh good," she said, taking in my empty plate. "You can help me carry out the mimosas."

I needed to talk to Grandma anyway. No way was I finalizing any deals with Xavier before that. "They're not really a mimosa crowd," I told her as we picked up the trays of flutes and headed toward the back door.

"As I've heard your friend Ant Eater remark on more than one occasion now, 'any booze is good booze,'" Hillary said primly as she nudged the door open with her knee. "If they don't like it, they can change the flavor of it like they did with the tea at your bridal shower. Oh yes," she added, arching her eyebrows at me as we headed out into the sunshine. "I know all about that now. At least they made mine champagne."

It was a gorgeous morning, warm but not hot yet, the sunlight filtering irregularly through the canopy of the sugar maples that rose like Roman columns in the backyard. I had always liked it out here—when I was ten I'd decided to camp in the gazebo for a week and made Hillary and Cliff help me set it up like a bedroom. He'd even dragged my mattress down for me, and Hillary had pinned sheets up around it to make it seem like a princess bed.

Huh. I'd forgotten that until just now.

Currently the gazebo was nothing like a princess bed, unless your idea of a princess was a lazy dragon snoring hard enough that the shingles vibrated. Flappy sprawled across the ornamental benches and let his head dangle over one of the handrails. Pirate was trying, without success, to cajole him into playing.

"There are tennis balls! Golf balls! *All kinds* of balls here!" he said, jumping over Flappy's tail as it swished back and forth. Aw, he must be dreaming. "You could try them all out if you just —Lizzie!" He noticed me and came running.

"No jumping!" I said when he got close. "I'm holding a lot of fragile things right now."

Frieda sidled up to me and lifted the tray out of my hands. "Not any more, you're not," she said with a wink, smirking around her cigarette. Despite the fact that she was walking around in a thigh-high electric blue kimono, Frieda's version of a bathrobe, her makeup was perfect. Maybe she'd had it tattooed. "I'll get these where they need to go. You go talk with Gertie." She nodded toward the toolshed on the periphery of the lawn, where I could see Grandma sitting on the seat of Cliff's riding lawnmower, talking with Ant Eater and Creely.

"Lizzie!" Pirate looked up at me with huge soulful eyes. "Why didn't you tell me you were having puppies?"

I choked on a laugh. "I'm not having puppies, I'm having babies," I explained as I headed for the shed. Pirate trotted along beside me.

"Puppies, babies, same difference," he said. "I'm going to love them so much."

I smiled at him. "Me too, buddy."

"And I can be your babysitter! I'll teach them everything they need to know about scent marking, and how to lick themselves thoroughly, and how to stand up to cats. It'll be great!"

"I'm sure you'll do your very best." And I would be right there in the same room the whole time. Just in case.

Grandma waved at me when I got close. She was already dressed for the day, in leather pants and a black T-shirt that read

Bikers Don't Go Gray: We Turn Chrome on it. "Good, you're up," she said, her voice rumbling like a diesel truck. "How's the ward?"

I held up my wrist and showed it to her. "Still working."

She grunted her approval and pushed a long strand of hair out of her face. "So, you talked to *him*."

There was no need to clarify. "Yep."

She glanced up toward the house. "What do you think?"

"I think he's a terrible person with a rotten track record," I replied frankly. "But...he makes a good case." He always did.

"Yeah." Grandma looked like she'd bitten into a persimmon. "He does. And I can't say that he's wrong, either."

Ant Eater chuckled from where she sat on a coil of rubber hose, sipping at a flute that had changed color from sunny orange to whiskey brown. "And Gertie's been trying to find a way to say that all morning." She waggled a piece of salami at Pirate, who snarfed it up eagerly. I resisted the urge to lecture her about appropriate treats again. It would never stick.

Creely had her head bent over a well-used pad of paper, a pencil stub sticking out of the corner of her mouth. "It's not a bad theory," she said, staring at her calculations. "And it's the only one we've found that gives Lizzie access to even a modicum of the power she'll need in order to tangle with a spirit."

"I was afraid of that." The witches would have handled it themselves if they could.

The quick wince on Grandma's face told me she felt the same. "Everything else we've come up with takes too much time to prepare, and that ward isn't gonna last much more than another day. If that."

I clutched the soft little bag, holding it tightly. A whisper ghosted across my mind, and I shivered.

He knew.

He was waiting.

"I can feel it," I told them. "We don't have long."

Grandma frowned. "It doesn't mean that your 'person of interest,'" she said, making finger marks, refraining from saying my father's name in case the spirit could be listening. "It doesn't mean 'he' holds all the cards," she said. "He's lost most of his mojo. He can't get you to the spirit realm on his own. To do that, we're going to set up a Cave of Visions."

"Mom mentioned that." I nodded. "Care to tell me why?" The last time we'd needed a ceremony like that, Grandma had told me they'd moved beyond it.

She shook her head. "The Seer's Ceremony is a hard one to control. Tougher still with a wild card like 'the great Satan' at the helm."

"Satan?" I asked. "Really?"

Grandma shrugged. "We need a nickname for him. Anyhow"—she placed a hand on my shoulder—"I want a reliable spell that minimizes the danger to you, and that means the cave."

"It's more manipulable too," Creely added. "Fewer variables to handle."

Fewer variables, right. Last time, they'd used everything from skulls to guppies to armadillo tracks to get the cave going. Honestly, the construction of these things was beyond me, but it didn't matter as long as they could make it what I needed.

I shivered, remembering the feeling of being sucked into the icy cold of the eleventh dimension by the succubus Serena. And now I was going to travel a place like that willingly, with only Xavier as my guide.

I had to be out of my mind.

A flute of orange juice appeared under my nose, held by a familiar hand. I took it and turned to Dimitri, who winked. "OJ and ginger ale," he said, "I hear it's good for morning sickness."

I exhaled my feelings of stress and smiled up at my husband. "Why, thank you."

He drew up next to me. "What's the good news?"

I took his hand in mine. "Grandma wants to make a Cave of Visions for me and you-know-who to use."

"The great Satan," Grandma supplied.

"That's a terrible idea," Dimitri stated.

"Your husband just has to get to know me," a familiar voice called.

Ah, and there was the man himself, swanning across the grass carrying his own flute, looking like he didn't have a care in the world.

"I'm sure that's not it," Dimitri fumed.

"All the players are here," Xavier continued. "Now we just have to hope your witches can build us a stable enough portal into the spirit realm," he added with a condescending nod to Grandma.

I could almost see the incantation dancing behind Grandma's lips. Her hand twitched toward her stock of Smucker's jars, but she stopped herself from throwing one. "We can handle our part if you can handle yours."

Dimitri grabbed Xavier's shirt and dragged him the rest of the way to our little circle. "You hurt Lizzie and you're a dead man."

"Ah," Xavier said, attempting to extricate himself.

Dimitri didn't make it easy.

"By the way, I'm going in with you," he said, shoving Xavier away.

I couldn't think of anything I'd like more, except…

Xavier was already shaking his head. "It won't work," he said, flinching, as if he expected Dimitri to grab him again. "I'm only strong enough to handle one passenger, and that has to be Lizzie. She's going to have to sever the connection to the spirit on her own."

"I can do it," I assured him.

Dimitri looked like he wanted to shout with frustration. "You're not the one I'm worried about," he said, his murderous glare on Xavier.

My husband turned to me. "For all we know, this plan is just a way for Xavier to try to take your power, same as the spirit."

Xavier sighed. The arrogance seeped out of him, and for a

moment he looked like nothing more than a tired, worn-down old man. "I understand that I've done things in the past with… questionable motives," he said, gazing straight at me. "I know you have very little reason to trust me. And that's fair, I deserve that. I never was the father you wanted, and I know damn well I'm not the father you deserve.

"But, Lizzie"—and there was an earnestness to his voice that wouldn't let me look away—"I mean it when I say that I'm only here to help. I *will* save my granddaughters and you, or die trying."

My breath caught. Granddaughters? I was having girls?

"How do you know?" Dimitri asked, his voice raw. "How do you know they're girls?"

Xavier's chuckle had a sad ring to it. "An angel always knows. I may be a shadow of what I once was, but even I can see that far."

Call it a mother's intuition, but I had a feeling he was right about the babies being girls. And Grandma seemed to think this plan of his just might work as well.

"All right," I said. I had my girls to think about now. I wasn't going to let them down. "I can do this if you can."

❧ 17 ❧

I wasn't exactly a newbie when it came to using the Cave of Visions.

Well, okay, that wasn't quite true. It wasn't a spell that *I* had ever cast, or that any individual witch could cast. It wasn't really a spell at all, more like a way to open a conduit to another plane of existence. It was supposed to be safer than just hopping through a portal and winding up in enemy territory, although to be fair, I'd done that with a Cave of Visions too.

It hadn't been my finest hour, but I'd lived to fight another day. That was pretty much my motto when it came to demon slaying.

The cave was different every time, but there were a few key components that stayed the same. One of them was that it took place in a small confined space, so when Grandma, Dimitri and I rolled to a stop that afternoon in front of a bowling alley, I wasn't quite sure what to expect.

Grandma pulled in next to me and popped her kickstand down.

I took my helmet off and shook out my hair. "Why here?" I asked her. "Why not a graveyard?"

We were trying to reach the spirit realm, after all. It made sense that we'd want to be where the spirits were.

Grandma scoffed. "Are you kidding me? After the shitstorm that went down in the last cemetery we tangled in, you want to go make yourself vulnerable in one? No way, Lizzie. Graveyards might be rife with spiritual mojo, but there's no telling how the people there died. With your luck lately, we'd end up tapping into the spirit of a mass murderer."

Oof. The truth hurt. "So you're saying this is where happy spirits hang out."

I recognized this bowling alley—twenty years ago it had been Billy's Bowling Bonanza, and a few of my classmates had thrown birthday parties here. I was a terrible bowler, and the pressure of performing in front of a bunch of judgmental preteens hadn't improved my game. Every ball I threw had been a gutter ball, even when the lane had bumpers—I'd thrown the ball so wonky once that it had skipped into the neighboring lane.

I'd spent the rest of that party locked in a stall in the bathroom.

Now the name was Flower Power's Bowl 'n Roll, but I still felt a residual rush of embarrassment just looking at it.

Grandma rolled her eyes. "It's got 'kinetic potential,'" she said, as if I should immediately agree. "Creely tested it. Cliff rented the place out for the day, and the coven started prep right after brunch while you two were otherwise occupied." She waggled her bushy gray eyebrows at us.

Yes, well, with the spirit knocking on my subconscious, I couldn't afford to get too close before the main event. We didn't want to tip him off. Besides—I glanced at Dimitri—I'd needed that distraction.

"My pleasure," he drawled, giving me a wink.

God, he was gorgeous. I hoped our babies got his eyes.

My hand was resting on my stomach before I even realized I'd moved it there. Dimitri covered it with both of his, pulling me into an embrace. The warmth of pure griffin goodness flowed through us, almost melting me into a puddle. I could stay like this all day.

"Get your rears in gear, lovebirds!" Grandma called out from the front door. "We've got less than an hour to defy the laws of space and time before that ward runs out!"

Right. I grabbed for the ward bag again, but holding it now wasn't as comforting as it had been a few hours ago. It quivered, the spells holding it together losing power by the minute.

I kept Dimitri's hand in mine and walked over to the bowling alley. "Let's see what's happening in here."

My mind was still my own, but I didn't know how much the spirit could see or hear. Grandma was right. It wouldn't be long before he pushed through.

Walking into Flower Power's Bowl 'n Roll was like crossing over into a hippie-slash-raver psychedelic concert hall. The overhead lights were off, but the black lights more than made up for it. Cartoon flowers in hot pink, lime green, and bright orange glowed under black light, festooning the walls, the chairs, even the alleys and bowling pins themselves. Underneath, subtle but there, hundreds of softly glowing white lines marked the floor and the lanes, swirling together like strands of DNA. The bowling balls looked like tiny planets all lined up, and the air was filled with the crash of scattering pins, the pings of the automatic scoring systems keeping track of who did what—and underneath it all, the unmistakable crackle of magic in the air.

Instead of sitting around meditating or chanting, witches bowled every lane. A few of them nursed beers. I thought I smelled nachos. In the distance, I heard Crazy Frieda cackle, "Seven-ten split, ladies! Who's yo mama?"

I picked my jaw up enough to speak. "What...the...hell?"

"Talk to Creely," Grandma advised, giving me a little push. "She's in the center lane. I've got to trade my boots for bowling shoes or we aren't going to get this thing off the ground." She gave me a small nudge. "It's all hands on deck."

Dimitri's hand tightened around mine. "I thought they'd be taking this a little more seriously," he muttered.

Me too. "There has to be a good explanation." I led the way to the center lane, which now that I got closer, seemed to be set up differently than the others. There *was* something like a cave here, a canopy of hundreds of white threads that glowed so brightly I had to blink to clear the stars from my eyes. Pinned between the threads were a bunch of random objects, everything from pictures to individual cigarettes to a do-rag with a laughing skull pattern on it.

"What the…" I drew closer to take a better look. One of the pictures seemed familiar. "Oh my gosh, I recognize him. That's Carl!" Carl was Frieda's hubby, dead and gone for longer than I'd known her. I'd met him once. He'd been a nice guy, for a ghost.

I carefully rounded the cave of twinkling threads, taking in each precious memory. Every item was a memento of a person we'd loved who had died—mostly Red Skulls, but I saw my fairy godfather's address book tucked against the bottom. Tears warmed my eyes. I hadn't been able to save Uncle Phil from the succubus in Las Vegas, but he'd promised he'd always be with me, watching over me. I felt it now.

Creely popped up next to me like a jack-in-the-box, startling the heck out of me. "Good, you're here," she said, ignoring my indignant gasp. "Watch where you step, okay? Don't smudge the lines, they're what's powering this whole thing."

Now that she mentioned it, I could see the connections between each thread of the glowing cave and the lines on the floor. It was like nothing I'd seen before, nothing I could have imagined in a million years. "How are they powering it? And why bowling?"

Creely nodded, her Kool-Aid red bangs bobbing around her eyes. "It's really quite remarkable. Think of it like this." She pushed her hair back. "We've got to conjure up enough power to get you and Xavier to the spirit dimension, right?"

So far, so good. "Yes."

"And then we've got to have enough energy saved up to keep you there long enough to sever the connection with the spirit."

Still following her. "Yep."

"Now, we don't know how long that's going to take. The last thing we want is for a witch to faint or a candle to burn out while you're stuck over there. It would be… disastrous."

"Yes, I'd like to come back," I agreed.

She nodded heartily. "Usually when we cast this spell, we juice it hard and fast. This time, though, we need something more like a battery." She waved at the gossamer tent.

"Powered by the connection to each person's spirit," Dimitri concluded.

"Exactly," Creely agreed. "Every bowler's ball is spelled to pass its energy, its sense of group and cohesion and spirit of the coven as it rolls down the lane. The energy is transmitted back to the cave along the spiral lines I marked out, and it all gets stored in this, our Cave of Visions, to be used by Xavier as needed. Think of it like…slingshotting your spirit across the dimensions, only the slingshot never entirely lets go."

I exchanged a glance with Dimitri. "I like it," I told her. Leave it to Creely to come up with exactly what I needed for any given job. She'd never let me down in the past.

Dimitri smiled as well. "It's good."

Creely cracked a grin and tucked a strand of her vivid red hair behind her ear. For once, her hair wasn't the brightest thing in the room. "Don't worry, the goat skull is waiting inside the cave."

"Sure." You couldn't forget that. I'd had it for every other vision quest. "Any guppies?" I asked. "Or birds, or heck, even a bunny or two right now?"

Creely snorted. "Consider Xavier your guppy."

Yikes. "That's not reassuring."

"We're flying by the seat of our pants," she admitted. "But it should work. Just…be careful."

"I always am," I promised.

I touched the nearest photograph. I thought it might be a young Betty Two Sticks—the crew cut was the same, even if her hair wasn't gray in the snapshot. She'd been careful as well, only it hadn't been enough.

"Where you're going, we can't follow," Grandma said, stepping down into the sitting area where the cave had been built. "But maybe the memory of our loved ones can. It'll be all right," she assured me, and herself.

I smiled as best I could.

I looked around, taking in all the activity with a new perspective. The witches bowled hard and fast, and I could see the cave get brighter and brighter. They were all working for this, for me. I was surrounded by my loved ones right now.

Even Hillary and Cliff were here, three lanes down, bowling with Ant Eater and Sidecar Bob. A quick glance at the score told me that, surprisingly, Hillary was kicking butt. Then again, if Hillary Brown was going to do anything, she was going to do it impeccably.

"Better get in there soon, Lizzie," Grandma said, looking down at the ward on my wrist. "I think you're about out of time." She pulled me into a hug. "Remember, no hesitating. Don't let it talk to you. You're there to kick ass, not take names." She let go and gruffly cleared her throat. "All right, clear a path. I need to get a ball."

Wait. "Where's Xavier?" He hadn't bailed, had he? If he'd run off...

"He's already inside the strands," Creely said, "meditating."

Interesting. I wasn't used to my father being quiet. I wasn't even sure he had the capacity not to talk himself up at every turn.

I was stalling, and I knew it. I took a deep breath and turned to Dimitri. He was worried. I felt it, even though it didn't show on his face.

"You've got this, babe," he said. His hands trailed from my shoulders to my waist, pulling me in close.

"I do." I had to. "We'll be fine. All four of us."

He laughed, but now I could see the glisten in his eyes. "Come here." He leaned down and kissed me hard, deep and rapturous, a glory of a kiss. I wrapped my arms around his neck and leaned into it for all I was worth. I wanted more. I could never get enough of my husband. And now we had a family.

We were both breathless when he broke the kiss. "You'd better leave before I can't let you go," he whispered.

"I love you."

"I love you too, Lizzie."

Burgeoned by the kiss, surrounded by my friends and family and the memories of our loved ones, I crouched down and crawled inside the glowing Cave of Visions.

Holy whoa…all the sound outside, the ringing and chatting and clatter of pins, it was all nonexistent in here. It was like stepping into the Matrix.

The bright white floor had a slightly ultraviolet glow under the black lights. Xavier sat cross-legged, his hands open on his knees, his eyes closed. I sat down across from him.

The goat skull stared up at me from where it was placed in between us. I stared at it for a moment and felt a little better. At least *something* about this ceremony was familiar.

"Lizzie." I glanced up and met my father's gaze. He appeared healthier than he had this morning, like being in the cave was recharging not just his power but also his vitality. I tried not to let that make me uneasy. He had to be strong if he was going to guide me to the spirit dimension and tether me there. "Are you ready?"

Ready as I'd ever be. I double-checked the utility belt around my waist. "What happens next?"

"Next, I need to connect with your spirit. Once I've got a grip, you'll release the ward bag. When the spirit appears in your mind, push toward it. Follow it back to its source. I'll make sure we don't get caught in any interdimensional whirlpools along the way."

That sounded bad. "What's an interdimensional whirlpool, exactly?"

Xavier smiled. "Nothing you'll have to worry about as long as you don't fight our connection."

Oh yeah, and he was making *that* real easy. "You sound a lot like the spirit, you know."

"Lizzie." He reached out with his hands, but didn't take mine. "I swear to you, I won't take anything from you. I'm only going along to give you a way back. I'll do everything I can to ensure your comfort with me—you'll hardly even notice I'm there." His smile went kind of lopsided. "And when this is all over, I promise, you'll never have to see me again."

Strangely, that didn't fill me with glee. But I could wonder about that after we got back. "All right." I took his hands. His grip was firm and dry. "Let's go."

"There's one last thing."

Just what I needed. "What's that?"

Xavier looked at me seriously, no smiles to be seen now. "Even with the coven's power, I'm not sure how long I'll be able to hold onto you. If I pull on the tether, you have to come back immediately, whether you've managed to cut the ties between you and the spirit or not. Otherwise, your spirit will be stuck there."

I'd figured as much, but it was more than a little scary to hear it laid out in black and white like that. I swallowed hard. "I understand."

"All right. Look into my eyes and try not to tense up."

I didn't even have a chance to wonder why I would get tense when, abruptly, the color washed out of Xavier's irises, leaving two filmy semicircles that stared creepily at me. His hands went cold, and a moment later mine did too. Veins stood out in his forehead and neck, black and pulsing. He looked like a dead man. I flinched.

"Just relax," he murmured. "Almost there…"

Suddenly the cold sensation of his hands in mine popped like a bubble. In fact, I couldn't feel his hands at all, even though I could see we were still connected. I didn't feel the pressure of my butt on the floor either, or my legs pressed together.

"Your consciousness has moved to your spirit, but your body will still respond," Xavier assured me. "Remove the ward bag."

I didn't think I'd have to. I could feel it suddenly give way, the fairy stone splitting in half. A second later, the spirit flooded back into my mind.

Elizabeth, really. He said, amused. *If you wanted to join me this badly, all you had to do was ask.*

"Push against it with your power, Lizzie!" Xavier commanded. I did, striking out with my demon-slayer powers. The spirit fell back easily—maybe *too* easily, but there was no time to second-guess myself.

It fled. And as if I was born to it, I pursued it across the dimensional plane. Xavier acted like a compass, gently nudging me when it seemed like I might careen into a patch of dark, bubbling green Hell or the livid purple of a corner of Purgatory.

I was doing it. I would catch the spirit, and when I did—

All of a sudden I felt myself tumbling head over heels, physically sensed it even though I had no physical form *to* sense. I tried to stabilize myself, but it was like being tossed around in a hurricane—there was nothing to hold onto, nothing to grope for, just the buffeting winds of fate or chance lashing at me until there was no up or down. I wasn't sure I could still feel Xavier's presence with me. I wasn't sure I could feel anything at all.

Hitting the ground with a *thump* a moment later was a rude awakening.

❧ 18 ❧

I hit the stone floor hard and groaned, rolling onto my side. I couldn't keep doing this while pregnant. At least right now, I hoped the babies were too small to feel the impact.

I pushed myself to a sitting position and found myself in a large circular room lit with narrow windows that let in anemic slants of light. The walls were stone, just like the floor, but they looked like sections of honeycomb, with hundreds of small holes carved into them. In each little niche lay what looked like a scroll, all of them tightly bound with bright red string.

Strange. I turned to look behind me, searching for the one feature I hadn't seen yet—a door.

There was nothing but more scrolls.

"Ah, Lizzie," purred the spirit, his voice clear. He was outside of me now. "You made it."

I swung toward the voice, one hand reaching down to my utility belt as I pushed myself to my feet. I didn't see anyone.

"Where are you?" I demanded.

Don't talk to him, Lizzie! Xavier's voice whispered a warning in my mind, but it was faint. I had the sudden, irrational thought that I was glad to hear from my dad.

At least he'd kept hold of me.

"Elizabeth, really." The spirit stepped forward out of the shadows. He had taken the form of a handsome, bald man, and he wore a tan robe that touched the ground when he walked. His lips quirked. "You know who I am. We've been getting to know each other for a while now." He spread his arms a little, smiling. It made him look like a viper flaring its hood. "Or is it just that you're surprised to see me in the flesh?"

I kept a hand on my switch stars. "You don't have any flesh."

That could be a real problem for me.

I snuck a quick glance at the tower room that had me trapped, noticing the thick parchment of the scrolls, the solid floor under my feet. Everything here *felt* real, but… "This is just an echo." It had to be.

"My dear Lizzie," the spirit crooned, as if he had a right to call me anything. "You are correct. His dark eyes followed my gaze. "In my earliest incarnation, I worked in the Library of Alexandria. It was one of the greatest repositories of knowledge ever to exist, and I was a cataloguer there. I had access to magic that no one today can even imagine." He inhaled slowly, deeply, and a breeze fluttered across the room.

It was as if he inhabited the entire space, as if everything in here were *him*.

He gave a small smile. The spirit was in no hurry.

He had me trapped.

"I had immense power at my fingertips. You know what that feels like, don't you, Elizabeth?"

"Don't include me in whatever sick game this is," I said. Only he already had. It was why I was down here, after all.

"So young," he mused. His expression darkened. "So arrogant." He took a step toward me, then another. "You see, Elizabeth, I was born without any special abilities, cursed to watch others fail to be all that they could be while heaped with gifts from the gods."

I gave no reaction, letting him talk, letting him get close.

"There are spells even the most hopelessly mundane can cast," he continued, "if you have enough *heart* for it." I really didn't like the rather murderous sound of that. He continued his advance. "Freeing my spirit from my mortal cage was one of them. Siphoning the spirits of my targets was another."

Great. He was like a teenager with a plastic tube, and I was a full tank of gas. He'd gotten close enough. I reached into my pouch for a spell jar, only to jolt when my hand passed right through it instead.

Amusement burst over his features. "You think you understand where you are, but you have no idea. Knowledge really is power."

He stepped closer, and I saw for the first time that what I'd thought was smooth skin was in essence more of a shell. Beneath his placid visage roiled dozens of others, new faces taking turns to press up against the glass like animals in a zoo, some gnashing their teeth, others screaming in silent rage and pain.

I felt my jaw drop. "Holy shit. What are you?"

"I am magic," he replied pleasantly, "and those are the spirits of my prey."

Cripes. He was his own portable Hell.

My throat tightened. I cleared my throat and spoke around it. "Who are they?"

"Friends," he mused. "Enemies," he added with a slight turn of the mouth. "Each one is connected to a scroll you see here, and each one lives on inside me. My own personal library of souls." He leveled his gaze at me. "You can learn to like it, Elizabeth."

"You're sick." He'd had one thing right. I never would have imagined this. Not in a million years.

I involuntarily took a step back, then another.

He kept advancing. "Once I was strong enough to have a choice, I went after the most unique and powerful individuals I could find. I wanted a biker witch," he mused, the corner of his mouth jerking up, "that is, until I saw you."

"You were trapped in Ant Eater's old family house," I countered.

He grinned. "Not trapped. Oh, Elizabeth, how you love to believe my stories."

Holy Hades. He'd been lying this entire time.

Speaking of it excited him. "Waiting for you, Elizabeth. You can be my crown jewel."

I sidestepped him. "We can work something out," I told him. "Maybe I could do a job for you." Something moral and upstanding.

As if this guy even knew what that meant.

He seemed delighted at my offer. "Some of my favorite souls tried to bargain." His voice hissed through the room like rain on a sidewalk. "Some tried to flee. The strongest tried to fight," he added, as if that excited him most of all. His face flushed and grew more transparent. The souls opened their mouths in silent screams. "No one can withstand me for long. I knew all their weaknesses, and now I know yours, Elizabeth Brown-Kallinikos."

As he spoke my name, his breath whispered through the room, creating a swirling gust of wind. It tickled my hair against my face and seemed to blow straight through me.

He drew close enough to kiss. "If you had only stayed on the other side, you could have at least bartered for your *own* life. But you came to me instead." He lowered his head and gazed up at me through thick, pitch-black lashes. "Now I will have all three of you. A half-angel demon slayer and her griffin-fathered twins." He licked his lips. "You're all so incredibly powerful. You will be the finest additions to my collection yet."

Holy crap. He had my number. And my power. And if I didn't play this right, he'd have my children and my immortal soul as well.

My father must have felt my panic.

Don't get caught up in his games. Just do it!

Right. I needed to get this party started. Only I had no idea how.

I grabbed up a switch star, willing it solid and deadly in my hand. It whirled to life, and before I could think, before he could read my mind and act, I jammed it directly into the spirit's chest.

Or I would have. A moment before contact, he vanished. My switch star passed through air and disintegrated from my hand.

He reappeared less than a foot in front of me, his hand around my throat. "That's it. Fight." His eyes twinkled. "It makes this much more fun."

Apparently he didn't realize I had more than one switch star. This one sliced right through his chest and up through the back of his head before he dissolved into nothingness.

The contact seared my arm and chest, like holding a live wire. I gasped and fell back.

He rematerialized on the other side of the room with a laugh. "You are fast," he said, like a parent praising a child.

Damn. That hurt. My heart pounded, and my entire body thrummed. I couldn't be risking electroshock while pregnant.

Had it even made a difference? I searched for damage. The spirit appeared whole.

That didn't mean I hadn't done some damage. I had to try again. Only my hand was numb as I reached for another switch star.

"You want to fight?" the spirit taunted. "We'll fight." A man appeared in front of him, dressed in furs and carrying an intimidatingly big ax. "Try your luck with a berserker. I've got plenty of souls who obey me."

Damn. I shook my hand out, desperately trying to get the feeling back. I didn't have *time* to take on his menagerie one by one; I needed to cut my tie to him *now*. Before I could figure out a way to get around him, the burly, ax-wielding maniac screamed and charged.

The emerald necklace vibrated, as if it couldn't quite get a move on.

Great.

Nothing worked in the spirit realm.

I let out a yell and hurled a switch star that slammed into the berserker's chest and stayed there, grinding. He kept charging.

The emerald necklace went liquid. Molten metal flowed down my arm and formed a saber.

To use against an ax-wielding maniac.

But I took the hint. I let out a yell and charged, meeting him halfway, sliding down onto my knees as soon as I came within striking distance and stabbing him in the gut.

He didn't even try to defend himself. The sword slid cleanly through his stomach. There was no blood, no guts, and after a garbled yell, he vanished into a ball of light that shot back into the belly of the spirit. It glowed upon contact and was swallowed up.

"Not the finest of Odin's warriors," the spirit said, his amusement evident. But I was already drawing a switch star and firing on him.

He disappeared again, and my switch star passed through the wall and into oblivion.

Damn.

"Why don't we try someone more magically inclined?" the spirit's voice crooned, from every direction at once.

I smelled smoke. I whirled around and saw an old man, gnarled wooden staff in one hand, a tiny pot of blue flames in the other.

What fresh hell was this?

Instead of throwing the pot at me, like I was expecting, he poured it over his head. Brilliant blue fire engulfed his body, so hot I could feel it from across the room.

"To an honorable death, demon slayer," he said then

attacked almost faster than I could track him. The flames trailed him like a cloak, and it was all I could do to remember that I could levitate. I swooped gracelessly into the air, barely missing getting tagged by his burning staff.

"Oh, don't be coy, Elizabeth." The spirit's voice surrounded us. "Go down and fight like a slayer. You won't let a simple shaman get the better of you, will you?"

There was nothing simple about this guy. Still, if *his* magic worked here, maybe I could pull this off.

I focused, thought hard about the sensations of my baby food spell jars, the weight of them in my hand, the coolness of the glass against my skin. I reached for my pouch again, and this time, I hit pay dirt.

Yes.

I grabbed a jar and hurled it at him, not even bothering to check what was in it.

It turned out to be an anti-energy spell, which broke against the shaman's head and poured over his face, cooling the fire as it went. By the time the drips reached his feet, the shaman wasn't just doused, he'd begun vanishing from the top down. After another few seconds, he popped into a ball of light and returned in a rush to the belly of the spirit who held him captive.

I barked out a laugh, half victory, half sheer, soul-deep relief.

"Clever." The spirit didn't sound so sanguine now. "But not clever enough. Let's see how you fare against your own kind."

❧ 19 ❧

My own kind? "You've killed other demon slayers?" I hissed.

He grinned. "More than I can recall." The scholar turned psycho pressed the tips of his fingers together. "Not all of them had spirits worth taking, but some were fierce enough to add to my collection."

And I would be forced to fight them all.

I was already breathing hard, my arm numb.

Not one, not two, but *three* new figures flashed into existence.

The first, a Japanese woman in a formal kimono, took a challenging stance with her naginata at the ready. The second looked like she'd stepped out of the Old West. She wore brown pants, a denim shirt, and a beat-up old bowler hat. Her hips cradled double gun belts, but she was way more deadly with a switch star in each hand. The final slayer was tall and muscular, with thick black dreads down to her waist. She carried a mambele, a huge half-knife, half-axe with a deadly curved blade at the front and a spike at the back. It crackled with lightning energy.

Oh my god. How was I going to survive them?

Lizzie… My dad's voice sounded faraway, weak. *I don't know how much longer I can hold you.*

I shifted just before the gunslinger's first switch star struck. Acid orange sparks exploded to my left, and I winced as a few of them burned me. I threw my star at her and swore as she ducked and dodged it.

The naginata swung in an arc toward my head, but my necklace surged up and into a helmet a nanosecond before it made contact. The racing metal stung, and the strike rang me like a bell, but it gave me time to throw another baby food jar. This one was a doozy—green and white, it went straight for the age-old slayer's throat. She grasped at her neck, eyes bulging as she began to choke. I grabbed another switch star and prepared to finish her off—

My necklace moved fast, but not fast enough to cover my leg before the mambele arced into it. I moved fast, but the tip grazed my thigh, and I shouted bloody murder as I chucked another switch star at the third slayer. It sheared through several of her dreads but didn't do any more damage, and she scowled at me as the mambele boomeranged back into her hand.

I went back to levitating in a hurry, pulling spells from my pouch and throwing them as fast as I could. My leg bled freely —not blood, which I'd been expecting, but drops of light.

That scared me more than anything.

It didn't hurt the way a wound like that should.

And every drop drained a little more of my energy. It was as if my life force was seeping out of me.

What did you do? my father's voice screamed in my head. *Your spirit is falling away. You need to finish this fast!*

"I can't," I panted, hurling a Paralyzing spell at the kimono-clad warrior. It hit her in a shower of silver sparkles, and I finally managed to nail her with a darn switch star.

She vanished in a burst of light.

What the fuck? I couldn't kill anybody. But they could drain me!

"I'm outnumbered!" I shouted at Dad, at the world. "He has too many ties for me to cut!"

Then just cut yours!

How? Where? There was no clear path, no simple way. In fact, it was becoming clear to me that if I wanted to escape this master spirit, I needed to get rid of every connection he had.

It was just as clear that I'd exhaust myself long before I managed that.

I needed help.

These slayers should be on my side, not his. "Who are you?" I demanded, dodging the axe end of the dreadlocked slayer's mambele. "And why the hell are you fighting for him?"

The gunslinger hurled a switch star at my head. I raised a hand and blocked it with my star. The impact threw me back against the wall, knocking the breath out of me. Sparks erupted as her star dropped away.

She glared at me, rivulets of sweat streaming down her face. "He has our names."

What? "That doesn't make sense." The dreadlocked slayer looked ready to take my head off when I said that.

"Read the scrolls," she hissed then cried out as her spirit captor struck her from behind. She fell hard, and in that moment, it all became clear to me.

The gunslinger shoved a switch star at my head. I levitated up; I shot to the ceiling, still incredulous. "You don't own your names." They were on the scrolls. "You've been erased." That was why I'd never heard of any of the other demon slayers. That was why no one told stories. The spirit owned them and their names and their entire identities. Without an identity, they were forgotten, lost to the ages.

I reached for the nearest scroll.

"Attack!" the spirit screamed.

Both slayers shot toward me.

"Atticus of Carthage!" I shouted, then shot down to the floor as switch stars and a mambele impacted the wall near where my head had been mere seconds before.

Metal rang out against stone as a red ribbon fluttered to the ground and a gleaming white soul shot out of the ancient scholar.

I had to read the names!

Hundreds of them.

I had to find my own.

Holy Hades.

"You can help me!" I hollered as the dreadlocked slayer's axe head caught my wrist. Light flowed freely—my life force.

"We cannot," she hissed, rearing back to strike again.

I hurled a switch star and she ducked. I shot to the other side of the room. I'd never survive long enough to find my name.

I searched desperately for someone, anyone. This was the spirit plane. Just because we were in a room that belonged to the spirit that had brought me here didn't mean there weren't others around. And if I'd ever had friends looking out for me on the other side—which I did—now was the time I needed them. I had to get to a window.

I threw a switch star at the slayer with the mambele, making her use it to deflect, then dodged right over her head toward the nearest slender window. It trembled, like it wanted to close in on itself, but I was fast. I groped for my pouch, yanked out the spell I thought would work best—and it hadn't escaped my notice that *here* all my spells worked way better than they did in the real world—and hurled it out the window.

The compulsion spell vanished into the nothingness that surrounded the room, but I *felt* it release its energy out there. It would call my friends to me if they were close enough and had my best interests at heart.

Not that I wanted anyone I cared about to be near this crazy spirit or this hellhole, but if there was a chance…if anyone was looking for me, well, now I'd lit a fire under their tails.

I just had to survive long enough for them to get here.

The mambele swooped in before I could move, slicing off a sliver of my shoulder. I was bleeding freely now. I wrenched my arm out of the window and smashed the side of my heavy bronze dagger square into the dreadlocked slayer's head. She staggered, dazed, and another switch star finished her off as well.

"Yes," the spirit clapped. "Well done. I'm so proud of all my souls."

Two more replaced the one I'd finished—a pair of twins dressed in flowing medieval dresses, like they'd walked straight out of a Caravaggio painting. Both flashed deadly smiles and drew massive swords.

I panted with fatigue, falling back against the wall even as my necklace became a Roman-style shield in front of me.

I had to keep going. My babies needed me—*Dimitri* needed me. He'd never get over it if I didn't come out of the Cave of Visions alive.

Don't think about that, Lizzie, just fight!

"I'm trying," I gasped, catching the next spear thrust on the edge of the shield. "How are you doing?"

Surviving, came my dad's answer.

He had to be getting tired as well. This was getting to be too much. I grabbed a spell and threw it at the pair of medieval slayers. It was a Macarena spell, of all things, but it hit one of them square in the chest. She grimaced, her heavy sword clanging to the floor as she began to dance, crossing her arms, swiveling her hips, and hopping away from me.

Thank God.

I reached behind me, my shaking fingers pulling out as many scrolls as I could manage.

Enriquo Vasqualiz! As I read the name, the paper disintegrated and the spirit gasped as a bright soul burst from his mouth and shot up and out the window.

Fingers trembling, I unrolled another and tossed the ribbon. *Gretchen Schmitt!*

The spirit staggered as the soul burst from his back, right between the shoulder blades.

The spirit had said it: Knowledge is power.

He raised his head, and for the first time, I saw fear.

His features hardened. "End it. Now," he ordered.

The remaining three attackers closed in around me. Countless others appeared behind them until the library was filled with souls the master spirit had claimed. His chuckle suffused the very air that I breathed.

"This is where it ends, Elizabeth. You did well," he said. "Don't worry. I'll cherish both you and your babies."

No! I braced the shield for all I was worth and drew a switch star.

"YEE-AAAW!"

The sound of a blessedly familiar yell broke through the tension, and a second later dozens of spirits poured through the windows and into the room, their swirling forms casting light, forming heads and legs and full-bodied biker witches.

Some of them rode hogs and some of them were on foot, but all of them were hollering to wake the dead. Spells began to fly, and I took advantage of the chaos and grabbed for more scrolls.

"*Lizzie McGee!*" I shouted.

The gunslinger exploded in a spray of light and energy.

I took refuge behind my shield. "Thank you," her voice whispered in my ear.

She was free.

I lowered the shield and saw the biker witches in full-blazing glory. I didn't even know all of them, but the ones I did recognize...there was Betty Two Sticks smashing jars over the heads of any spirits she could reach. I saw Lazy Rita and Lucinda the Lush—Rita threw Paralyzing spells like confetti, and Lucinda tossed Molotov Cocktail spells onto the heads of my attackers. There was Easy Edna and Battina and Carl—

A goth slayer with a tear-drop tattoo tossed switch stars double handed.

"Phoenix?" I gasped. No, it couldn't be her—my birth mother had given up her birthright and passed her demon-slaying power on to me and was alive and dull as far as I knew. So this had to be...her twin sister. "Aunt Serefina!"

"Lizzie!" she called out cheerfully while bashing the goth slayer over the head with a Mind Wiper. "Good to finally meetcha, kid."

The goth slayer's eyes went dull for a moment, then lit up like this was the best day ever.

"I've always wanted to be on *American Idol!*" the slayer gushed as the Mind Wiper filled her head with her greatest fantasy.

"Hold them off while I read the scrolls!" I called to the witches.

Serefina gave me the thumbs-up before tossing another spell. She threw them like they were Frisbees, slicing through spirits left and right. She ducked under a scimitar, slung a spell at a spirit that made it swell up like a balloon, and then said, "On your left!"

I turned just in time to dodge the remaining medieval slayer's sword.

"We're on the same side!" I yelled. "You don't have to do this!"

She drew back, jaw tight. "I don't have a choice," she gritted out. "And neither will you if you don't end him." Her features wavered for a moment, like something else was pushing against the inside of her body. Her hands shot forward, and a wave of power slammed into me, knocking me onto my back.

Lizzie! I felt my father's agitation, his growing fear, but there was nothing I could do to reassure him. The impact knocked the air out of me, and before I could recover, she was there, one leather-sandaled foot stomping hard on my right hand. She raised the broken spear up high, but before she could bring it down, her whole body blurred. She was frozen in place, the master spirit locked in combat against the slayer's own will.

I thrust up with my left hand, trusting the bronze necklace to come through for me. It did, and a moment later my sword formed just in time to slide through my attacker's chest. She dropped her spear and began to slump.

"Tell me your name," I demanded. "I'll say it."

A victorious smile crossed her lips. "You'll find it." She vanished before she hit the ground.

The master spirit's anger suffused the room like an electrical storm, crackling and driving his captives to even greater efforts.

Scarlet plugged a Moorish warrior with a Giggle spell then reached behind her for a handful of scrolls. "*Clarence Barton, Imidi Rhoos, Saanvi Patel!*"

The spirit reeled.

"*Yu Yan Zhao, Sasha Ivanov, Kelly Fletcher!*" Battina hollered from the other side of the room.

Souls burst free.

The spirit's attack crumbled as one by one, the warriors burst into light and energy—free.

"It's working!" The biker witches and me; dead or alive, we made a hell of a team.

Serefina grinned at me. Then I watched her face fall as a cold hand gripped my arm, and suddenly everything went dark.

❦ 20 ❦

We stood alone in a void, the spirit and me. It appeared to be the ocean at night, but I knew better. The water lapped up to my ankles, the cold of it seeping up my legs. Water as far as the eye could see.

"Impressive," the master spirit said, his face flushed. "I underestimated your creativity, Elizabeth, and the emotional investment of your coven. You cost me a great deal, but at least I have you."

He held a scroll in his hands. Mine, I was sure of it.

I reached for it, and it disappeared into nothingness.

"You can't say your own name." The corner of his mouth tugged up. "And there is no one here who will say it for you."

He'd taken me away from my friends, from the witches, from anyone who could help me.

He took a step closer. "You will help me rebuild my collection." He reached for me. "Now the time has truly come. Don't be afraid. You'll like being mine."

I glared at him, defiant even though I knew there was no point. Inside, I felt the tether to Xavier struggle and tug. I was surprised he'd held on this long. I didn't want him to feel bad when he lost our connection. There was nothing else he could have done. Nothing I could do anymore.

"Yours will be the first children I have," the spirit gushed. He closed in on me. "I will name them, and then there is no way they will ever be able to escape me. They and their power will know nothing but me. Soon, even you will forget that you ever had a life outside of my mind." He raised his hands, and the spirits alongside him tensed. Slowly, keenly, I felt him touch the edge of my soul.

"No," I whispered. But I knew there was no way left to fight him.

The tug in my head became a full-on ache, and with a sudden burst of pain, the void filled with a light brighter than anything I'd ever seen before. I winced and closed my eyes, even though every instinct I had screamed for me to be on alert, on attack.

A gentle touch to my arm brought me out of it.

"Lizzie."

I opened my eyes to see my father standing between me and the spirit, but this—this wasn't the Xavier I'd left behind in the Cave of Visions. This was a being of pure energy, completely untainted by the demonic influences he'd carried as long as I'd known him.

This was Xavier the angel. "I thought I'd lost all chances of coming back to this side. But feeling you in pain, knowing I had to be something different…" He took my hand. "I think I can do this." Doubt flickered across his drawn features. "I hope I can."

I gaped.

He smiled and unfurled a pair of wings. Xavier's gaze held mine, as if he was still getting used to the change himself.

"I never thought I could be this again," he told me, his pearlescent wings blocking the spirit like a shield.

"Watch out," I said as the spirit lunged for him. His hands passed straight through my father, and both gasped.

I reached for my father. Speaking hurt. Moving hurt. My spirit was so tired and aching that all I wanted to do was lie down and pass out.

Xavier folded his wings and turned to face the master spirit.

"Be gone, angel, this doesn't concern you," the spirit snapped. "Your powers are almost spent."

Xavier nodded. "That's true. I'm not strong. And I've never been as noble as I should. I won't make it out of this. But neither will you."

"Say my name," I said to my father. "All of it."

"Elizabeth Gertrude Brown Kallinikos," he said, as proud as any father could be.

The spirit stumbled as my name escaped him, and I saw a red ribbon flutter to the surface of the dull, black water.

I reached down for a switch star and felt it hard and solid in my hand. It began to churn. The spirit glared at me. Instead of the tall, intimidating figure I first saw, he seemed bent and frail now.

"You should never have threatened me," I ground out. "You should *definitely* never have threatened my children." I raised my switch star. "Enjoy oblivion, asshole." I threw it, and it cut right through the spirit's head. He fell apart like he was being unzipped.

Bright light burst from him as the spirits of those he had captured shot forth, free at last. It was beautiful. There would be no more names to read, no more souls captured. No more torment and pain from that monster.

The two halves of him fell away. And just as I breathed a sigh of victory and relief, the void itself crumbled with him.

"Yikes!" I was falling. Until I wasn't. I hung in the middle of nothing now, surrounded by the vast emptiness of the spirit realm. The only point of contact I had was Xavier, who held me by my shoulders. His wings, so bright only moments ago, were fading quickly, and so was the rest of him. "Dad!" I hollered, looking for some guidance. A bit of reassurance.

"It's time for you to go back," he ordered.

That seemed like a great idea. "Let's go."

Xavier shook his head. "Get your spirit tended to fast, Lizzie. You're leaking everywhere."

"Shouldn't you be doing that?" I barked, trying to absorb what he was saying.

"I've done all I can." He smiled down at me, sad yet more fulfilled than I'd ever seen him. Light shone from his entire being, and he almost appeared...happy. "I love you, pumpkin. I always did." He paused. Cringed. "I just wasn't good at being good."

Oh, my god. "You're leaving me."

He shook his head, a rueful gesture. "It has to be this way. I can't go back in this form, and I am fading."

"But—" I began.

His eyes held mine. "I'd give anything for it not to be this way. I swore I'd do better this time. I swore I'd never leave again. But this time, I really do have to go."

"You saved me," I told him. "You saved your grandbabies."

He lit up at that. "They saved me back." Then, through eyes welling with tears, he added, "Go now."

He pushed me away. The winds that had carried me here rose out of nowhere.

Before I could say anything else, the hurricane swept me away, tumbling me back toward the physical world and leaving Xavier, the last of his power diminished from a tether to a tiny thread, to watch me go.

M y dad was gone.

He'd sacrificed himself for me. He'd tried to use the last of his powers to get me out, and…the wind pushing me away, back toward the Cave of Visions, slowly died down.

Then it stopped altogether.

I hovered in…nothingness. White surrounded me. Wispy shapes, like clouds, formed here and there in the distance. Otherwise, I was completely alone.

I felt the last of Xavier's powers give way, thinning from little to nothing until, with a pop I felt like a last gasp inside my chest, he was gone. Xavier, my father, my *tether*, was gone, and I was trapped.

Nausea stirred in my belly, and I placed a hand there. The babies. They were trapped here with me. We were supposed to be back in the Cave of Visions. I'd defeated the spirit. Well, Dad and I had. And the biker witches. Everyone had come through for me, and in the end, Dad just didn't have enough power to get me back.

I was alone, adrift, and terrified.

There was nothing around me, nothing at all. No

landmarks, because there was no land. No distinguishing colors, because everything was the same flat, hollow white in every direction. There wasn't even a breeze anymore, nothing to push me back toward the realm of the living.

I pumped my arms, as if swimming would help. It didn't.

Oh, my god…Oh my god…

I had no idea how to move, and even less of an idea about where to go if I could. How did you pick between left and right when there was no real difference between them?

My heart beat like a snare drum in my chest, sounding louder in my ears than it had any right to. I stretched out with all my limbs, trying to feel anything, anything at all, but— nothing. I tried to turn myself around, to swivel and roll like I was back in the windstorm of Xavier's power, but it was impossible. There was nothing to push off of, nothing to use as a catalyst.

Grandma had said point-blank she couldn't get me back.

It had been up to my dad.

And now?

I strained to see past the dull white of nothing.

"Scarlet!" I hollered, my voice barely registering. The sound here was muted. As if there was nowhere for it to go. "Battina! Any Red Skull!" I tried.

I yelled until my throat went hoarse.

It seemed my dad had gotten me closer to home, but certainly not close enough—they couldn't hear me.

"No," I whispered. It wasn't going to end like this. It couldn't. After everything I'd just gone through, all the fights and the showdown and Xavier's death, I wasn't going to go down stuck in the middle of nothing. "No!"

I reached out with my power, which made every spirit wound on my body pulse like I'd been doused in acid. It didn't matter—pain was temporary, but if I couldn't get out of here, then I'd be looking at an eternity of emptiness, and that just wasn't an option. I had Dimitri to think about and Pirate and my parents. I had my babies to think about.

Oh god, my babies. I couldn't stay here. I had to get home!

I knew that panicking wouldn't get me anywhere, but fighting it down felt almost as hard as defeating the master spirit. It took too much time, but eventually I calmed my rat-a-tat breaths and brought my heart rate down from "Led Zeppelin" to "Ringo Starr" levels. There had to be a way out of this. I just needed to find it.

Maybe I could summon up my own wind. I didn't have a destination, true, but if I was lucky, I'd blow myself to a solid place then find my way back to the physical realm from there.

I mean, I'd been lost in purgatory before. I could do this.

I closed my eyes and envisioned the hurricane feeling that had wrapped me up so strongly before. I was half angel. If Xavier could summon a gale, I should be able to get a breeze going.

I felt a stirring. Just a hint, but it was enough to give me hope. I poured my energy into it, shouting with joy as I began to tumble again.

But the spin stopped almost as quickly as it began.

I frowned and opened my eyes. Then I caught sight of my body and gasped with horror. My wounds had gone from dripping drops of silver light to looking more like faucets, draining me dry. Hadn't Xavier just warned me about getting my spirit tended to soon?

I let go of my effort completely, so frustrated I wanted to cry. I couldn't push too hard, because then I'd drain myself of everything that still sustained me. If I *didn't* push, though, I'd be stuck here, because I knew that the coven wouldn't be able to find me in this nowhere place. It was a miracle I'd gotten the help I had from the Red Skulls who'd already crossed over. I wished I weren't so far away. The Red Skulls always had a plan.

"I'll figure this out." I had to believe that. Something would come to me, but in the meantime...I hurt, every inch of skin stinging like I'd rolled in a field of nettles. I had overextended. I needed to rest for a moment, just rest. I'd try again in a minute.

I closed my eyes again and wrapped myself up in a hug. I could barely feel the solidity of my own body anymore. No spell jars clanked in my pouch, no switch stars dangled at my side. There was only me surrounded by all of this emptiness. It was almost beautiful, in a terrible way. Almost…tempting. The pain started to fade, and I sighed with relief. I'd get going again in a minute. Just one more minute…

But in my heart, I knew that was just a fantasy.

I'd saved the others, but I couldn't save myself. I'd never see Dimitri again. I'd never feel his arms around me, never see his smile. We'd never get to cuddle on the couch together as our babies slept on his chest. I'd never watch our daughters fly with him, clinging to his back as he soared over the yard. They'd never mash peas on his shirt. He'd never read them a bedtime story, all curled up in bed together.

I felt a surge of love and loss, and the answering whisper of Dimitri's energy.

"I'm sorry," I whispered. The only thing I'd ever really wanted was to be a family.

A surge of heat in the center of my chest shocked me out of my stupor. I reached for the source instinctively, and my hands clasped my emerald necklace, the one Dimitri had given me to protect me. The bronze chain had gone from warm to hot in a hurry, and I knew for a fact that it wasn't responding to anything I'd done.

Was I about to be attacked again? I didn't think I could take another battle.

I could barely lift my head to search for the coming attack.

One second I was alone, and the next—oh, the next—the most beautiful sight in the world swooped into existence in front of me. A griffin, my griffin!

Dimitri's wings flared in a dazzling rainbow display of raw Mediterranean heat and power. He flew toward me at breakneck speed, and his piercing cry broke the cottony silence of the spirit realm.

"Dimitri!" My voice sounded muffled even to myself, but he arched his back in joy.

He swooped to my side, and it was the best feeling in the world when I wrapped my arms around his neck. Like coming home.

He was warm, as warm as the emerald he'd given me to keep me safe. I felt whole again, loved. And I sighed with utter relief as I climbed onto his back and felt his solid bulk supporting me. I clung to his neck as his wings began to pump. I gave in to the feeling of him under me as we began to move together.

There was no wind this time, just a slow rise like stepping out of the ocean and back onto dry land. We rose until the white became gray, then black. We rose until everything faded away...

I blinked my eyes open and saw sunlight—beautiful, dappled sunlight shining through a familiar window over my head.

Holy hand grenades, I was back! And I wasn't alone— Dimitri lay in my bed with me and held me close to his chest, his arms locked in an embrace. He felt like he might never let me go. I was just fine with that.

"Hey, babe," I whispered. Dimitri shivered.

"Oh, thank God, Lizzie," he said, his chest rumbling against my cheek. He bent and kissed me long and hard before he tore himself away. "How are you feeling?"

Better now. I took stock of my body curled up next to him. "Tired, but good." I stretched my legs. "Surprisingly good." It was such a relief to be back home, with him.

He let out a short chuff. "Let's agree to never, ever do that again, all right?" He sounded wrecked.

I snuggled deeper into his arms and kissed his collarbone. "I can get behind that idea. But at least you found me." I'd been afraid no one would.

Grandma let out a groan. "'But you found me,' she says," Grandma mimicked, as acerbic as a whiskey sour. "The boy's insane. Good thing, too."

I rolled over to see her. "Hey, Grandma. We did it."

She didn't look happy. In fact, my bedroom was filled to the brim with frowning witches. Hillary was with them, perched on the vanity stool, wearing a Ralph Lauren pantsuit and a worried expression.

Oh no. "What went wrong?" I asked. "Besides the fact that I almost faded into nonexistence in a place of pure existential dread."

I sat up and realized I had a headache and was a bit woozy. Still, it could have been worse. It *had* been so much worse.

"You're crazy," Grandma said flatly. It took me a minute to realize she was talking to Dimitri, not me. Her harsh gaze turned on me, as if she couldn't quite believe I was whole and sitting there. "Don't get me wrong, I'm sure as hell grateful he found you, but there's no way that should have worked."

"Xavier is gone," I told her. "The spirit had too many lackeys for me to fight alone." We'd both taken a beating. "My dad used his last energy to try to get me home. It wasn't enough."

She lowered her gaze to the floor. "I know." She shook her head. "We warned him he'd die if he kept it up." She looked up at me, her eyes glazed with tears. "He said he was done failing; that he'd give anything for you and the babies." She gave a shrug. "I didn't know he had it in him."

"He came to me in the other realm," I said. I hoped he knew I'd made it back. After all he went through at the end, not knowing just seemed too cruel.

She nodded. "We thought we'd lost you." She snorted. "Then your idiot husband refused to wait for us to even come up with another way to reach you."

He stiffened behind me. "There was no time." He wrapped his arms around me from behind, supporting me. "I saw Xavier die, and I felt his connection to you break. I knew your spirit would be lost if we left you like that, so I took his place."

"Damn fool," Grandma said, but there was no heat to it anymore. "He went by *feel*, if you can believe that, Lizzie. Like feelings are some sort of compass."

Dimitri rubbed my arms. "I had to do it. I wasn't about to lose you and our babies without doing everything I possibly could to get you back. If I failed, at least then I wouldn't have to live without you."

Oh my god. He'd thought he was watching me—us, his *family*—die. I squeezed his arms around me. "I'm so grateful you found me," I said, turning to him. "Still, I'd never want you to die for me."

He kissed my hair, one arm rubbing soothingly down my back. "Good thing it's not up to you, then," he remarked. "And it really wasn't as dangerous as they're making it out to be."

"Oh no?" Ant Eater rolled her eyes. "You wanna share how throwing your spirit into the deep end of the pool without knowing how to swim ain't dangerous?"

Creely rolled her eyes. "It's why portals were invented," she said impatiently. "So you don't get stuck between dimensions."

Dimitri gave a small chuckle. "Lizzie and I are connected by more than love and marriage," he said. His thumb rubbed across the emerald necklace's bronze chain at the back of my neck. "Our spirits are connected as well. I know what she feels like inside and out. I could find her in a snowstorm or a blackout or across dimensions."

Oh, my word. He was so unlucky the biker witches were here. If we were alone, I'd show him exactly how his words made me feel.

"It explains how you found her," Grandma said, crossing her arms over her chest. "But how did you get her back?"

"Ooh la la," I said, snuggling closer to him. "You did something so cool the biker witches don't know how to do it."

I could hear the smile in his voice. "I followed my clan

Helios bonds. I've always been strongly connected to my sisters —you all know that."

Did we ever. They were the reason he'd come after me in the first place—he'd needed a slayer in order to save them from a demon's curse. He'd ended up falling in love and staying for my sake. His sisters were still hugely important to him.

"All I had to do was follow the worry," he continued, sounding more amused than upsetting his sisters like that probably merited. "And the swearing."

"That was a hell of a thing to gamble on, honey," Frieda said from the back, cracking her gum like a whip. Her eyes were soft, though. "But I hear you. Nobody wanted to think about livin' in a world without our Lizzie in it."

Our Lizzie. I was theirs, really theirs, friend and family and more, and they were mine. The way I'd managed to summon the coven to help me had proved that. For a good portion of my life, I had wanted more family than I'd had. I'd convinced myself that Hillary and Cliff were disappointed in me, and that everything would be better once I was back with my real family. That had been a mixed blessing, to say the least, but now— finally—I thought I'd figured out the truth.

Family was so much more than who you were born to. Family was who raised you, who cared for you, who kissed your cheek before putting you to sleep, and who taught you to ride a bike. Family was a group of crazy witches who would follow you to Hell and back—literally—and fight to keep you safe. Family was the person who loved you more than anyone else in the world and would do desperate things in the name of that love. For me, family was even my birth father.

Oh, Xavier. I hoped he'd gone back to where he'd fallen from, in the end.

I brushed a tear away with the back of my hand and looked up at my husband. "Thank you for protecting me."

"Always." He gazed at me like I'd hung the moon. *"Always,* Lizzie." He leaned down for a kiss, and I stretched up to meet him. Our lips touched, and the love that poured through my body made me shiver with pure contentment. Everything I'd been missing about the spirit realm, the strength of a true connection, was right here. This was no echo, no shadow of what had once been—this was my husband in my arms, real and solid and wonderful.

Someone whistled. Someone else—Creely, I thought—started making predictions about how long the kiss would last. I ignored it all until—

"A*hem*."

Oh jeez. I'd forgotten my mom was here. I could handle the witches catcalling me, but my mother was another matter entirely. I broke the kiss and glanced over at her. She had a glass of water in one hand and her cell phone in the other.

She smiled and handed me the water. "Well, I'm very glad you're feeling better, Lizzie. However, you *did* just endure a rather traumatic experience. It's probably not a bad idea for you to make sure you're hydrated. You also need to go to a hospital and get checked out."

Ugh, *hospitals*. I took a sip of the cool, clear water. It tasted so good I polished the whole thing off in one long pull. "I think I'm fine, Mom," I said once I was done.

"That's nice," she began. Yikes. That was what she always said when it wasn't nice at all. "But there's more involved in this than just *you* these days, honey." She glanced down at my abdomen. "We want to make sure the babies are doing well. And," she added, with a twinkle in her eye, "they'll probably want to do an ultrasound, which means baby pictures!"

❧ 22 ❧

One doctor's visit later, I found myself lying in a hospital bed with an IV in my wrist. It wasn't serious—"mild anemia and dehydration" according to the doc, but since I had to get an ultrasound anyway and Hillary was in charge of things, that meant a private room, rehydration therapy, and a ton of visitors.

Personally, I was willing to endure anything just to be alive and whole—and with my family.

Still, it was a darn good thing the wide, beige-and-blue room was private, all things considered. Most of the witches had already been in and out, bringing in everything from anatomically correct balloons that spelled CUMGRATULATIONS STRAIGHT SHOOTER! to a perfume atomizer from the gift shop that had been repurposed as a spell sprayer.

They were more slaphappy than they usually were after a victory. I'd told them about their friends on the other side, how well they were doing. How they'd helped. Even Ant Eater's eyes had welled with pride.

Then she'd stepped back, gotten busy, and warded the heck

out of the room. That meant no one that was even having a bad day wanted to come anywhere near the place. On the negative side, the spell contained skunkweed, which—yeah, nasty. Pirate had gotten so excited by it that Frieda had had to take him for a walk just to clear his nose. I could see them out the wide window to my right, in some trees past the parking area, searching for the perfect spot.

"Oh my goodness." Hillary's pale pink heels clicked on the tile. She still hadn't put down the picture the doctor had printed off from the ultrasound. In fact, she'd gone and put it in a silver Tiffany frame that she'd had stashed in her purse. Yes, in her *purse*, because who knew when you'd need to immortalize something in fashionable silver? That was my mom. She bent her head over the photo, the feathery ends of her blond bob grazing her chin. "Look at those little heads just nestled together! They're so sweet!"

"They are," I said, welling with pride. I couldn't wait to meet them.

Ant Eater took a look over Mom's shoulder. "They look more like aliens than babies," she announced, scratching her head under her Red Skull do-rag. "Slits for eyes, tiny flailing limbs...creepy."

Hillary, to my complete surprise, didn't jump down Ant Eater's throat. She just laughed. "They're only ten weeks along, you can't expect them to look like actual babies yet. But this is the first picture of many." She closed her eyes and hugged —*hugged*—the frame. "I'm so excited! Oh, Lizzie, Dimitri." She looked at me expectantly. "*Tell* me I can host the baby shower for you. I've got the perfect place all picked out."

Oh my. "Where is that?" I asked, my grip on Dimitri's hand tightening a little. He sat next to me on my bed, arm around my shoulders, keeping me close. He had barely let go of me since I woke up. I kind of liked it.

"The country club has a brand-new ballroom opening up next spring, right next to their gardens! It's already booking up, but I've got enough pull to get us a reservation there any time you want."

A country club. Hoo-boy. "I'm not sure we're really that kind of crowd," I told my mom gently. Heck, just imagining the things the witches might get up to in my parents' staid and prissy country club made me want to reach for a bucket full of Mind Wipers. We'd need them.

Before Mom's face could fall, though, Ant Eater piped up. "I kind of like it." She nudged Hillary. "I've always wanted to party in a posh place like that."

"Oh, you will just *love* it." Hillary patted her on the nudgy elbow while simultaneously taking out her phone. "The club is beautiful and completely refurbished and also very heavily insured against accidental damages! Let me show you the pictures." She glanced at me. I must have worn my disapproval on my sleeve. "Here." She tugged Ant Eater toward the door. "Come out into the hall with me for better light."

I turned to Dimitri. "And I thought it was a miracle when you pulled me from the void."

Grandma snatched the frame from Mom's hands as the door flapped behind the unlikely baby shower planners. "You know once those two decide, there ain't no un-deciding," she remarked, making her way over to the bed. She settled in next to us, looking at it with an odd expression.

"I never saw pictures like this of my girls," she said, tapping the frame with one long finger. "Probably for the best. Phoenix and Serefina spent so much time smacking into each other in there, I doubt a doctor could have even gotten a steady pic of 'em."

"Serefina looks good," I said. I'd told her all about our encounter.

"Yeah." Grandma flushed with pride.

Still, I felt for her. Looking back had to be rough. One of her daughters was dead, and the other was a coward who'd abandoned everything her mother had tried to teach her. I groped for something else to say.

Grandma chuckled before I could get a single word out. "They were little hellions as toddlers. Never slept at the same time—one would be napping and the other would be caterwauling at the top of her lungs. And oh, you haven't lived until you've tried to feed, change, and soothe two babies at once, let me tell you!" She turned a grin on me that looked inordinately gleeful.

She scratched absently at the tattoo of a phoenix on her arm. "Pregnancy is a beautiful thing, kiddo, but swollen ankles, a sore back, disgusting food cravings, and giving up your entire wardrobe for months ain't the greatest. Lucky for you, you've got all of us around to lend a hand."

"Heavens to Betsy." I hadn't considered that. I turned to Dimitri, hoping I didn't look as shell-shocked as I felt. "She's exaggerating, right?"

Dimitri wasn't quite smiling, but I could see he wanted to from the way the corners of his eyes creased. "Actually, from what I remember of my sisters as babies…no, she's pretty much right on." He tugged me closer. "We're not going to be getting a lot of sleep for a few years. But," he continued as my mouth dropped open, "we'll have plenty of help—probably more than we want, honestly—and it'll all be worth it."

"Yeah?" I raised an eyebrow playfully. "Are you planning on being this lovey-dovey with me when I've got a belly out to here?" I stretched the arm that wasn't attached to an IV out in front of me.

Dimitri did smile this time. "Even more so," he promised. "More every day." He bent, about to kiss me, but then his phone beeped. "Hang on." He checked the text message, and his expression fell. "Oh, shit."

"What?" I demanded. He didn't say anything, so I poked him in the side. "What?"

My big bad griffin fought back a cringe. "My sisters are—"

"Lizzie! Dimitri!" The door flew open and twin tornadoes hurtled through like the place was on fire. Diana and Dyonne had arrived, almost as colorful as their griffin forms in red and blue sundresses and yellow sandals.

Oh my. "Aren't they supposed to be in Greece?"

"Santorini," Dimitri remarked dryly.

Not that I was complaining.

"Surprise!" Diana exclaimed from the doorway.

Dyonne pushed past her, her arms loaded with shopping bags. "We have had plans for months to come out for your birthday." She handed a bunch of bags to a startled Ant Eater. "Then all this craziness happened, and you had us worried sick."

Dimitri's sisters dodged my meal tray and a cardboard cutout of a doctor that the witches had snagged from the gift shop. They came at me in a flurry of jostling elbows and dropped packages before making it to my bedside.

"It's a great surprise," I said, accepting hugs and congratulations.

Diana pushed a long dark strand of hair out of her face. "Dimitri didn't make it easy," she said, and when Dimitri opened his mouth, she added, "Why else did you think Dyonne was so pushy about getting details from you?"

"General female nosiness?" Dimitri offered.

"Not this time," Dyonne said.

"We were focused on other things." Diana grinned.

"Like giving the plane a little bit of assistance with a tailwind on the way over," Dyonne supplied with a Mona Lisa smile designed not to give anything away. Her short layered hair did seem a bit windblown. "The pilot said it was the fastest time he'd ever clocked from Athens to Atlanta."

"How fast?" Dimitri asked, not amused.

"Does it really matter?" Dyonne waved him off. "That's all in the past now!" She put her hands on her hips. "What *matters* is you freaking us out long distance, while we were at the airport, and then not even bothering to pick up the phone when we landed. I called from the tarmac, the tarmac!"

"I texted," Dimitri shot back, a little halfhearted.

"Oh, what, *this* text?" Diana turned on her phone and read straight from it. "'Lizzie and babies safe, don't worry.' And I said, what? This is the first mention we've had of any babies, and *then* what have you done when I try to call? You've turned your phone off!"

Dimitri shifted uncomfortably against my side. "Lizzie was sleeping. I didn't want to wake her."

Diana threw her hands up in the air. "Lizzie and babies! And *babies*! What—you—how could you just—" She exhaled hard, shook her head, then sat down on the other side of my bed, which was getting pretty tight at this point. "Are you okay?" she asked seriously.

"I'm fine," I assured her. "There was a bit of a throwdown—"

"In a manner of speaking," Grandma added.

"But it's all handled now!" I finished cheerfully. "This is just to get me rehydrated. We'll be out of here in an hour, probably."

"So everyone is all good?" Dyonne practically bounced up and down with excitement. "Do you know what you're having yet?"

"Girls." The ultrasound hadn't been definitive, but I knew Xavier had been right. "We're having baby girls."

"Eeeeeeee!" Matching squeals and hands on faces made Dimitri's sisters look like teenagers. I grinned while he winced.

"Oh my gosh, this is perfect, and I brought the most amazing presents," Diana exclaimed. "They were going to be presents for you, brother, but you've been demoted. We're giving them to the babies."

"They're out in the car with Antonio," Dyonne added. "We thought they were a little too big to bring into the hospital."

"What are they?" I asked at the same time Dimitri said, "Antonio? Antonio who?"

"Not *that* Antonio, the *other* Antonio," Diana assured him. "The one with the Pegasus breeding program? It's brilliant. He's got a fantastic stud with a wingspan of over—"

"Saddles," Dyonne interjected with an eye roll. "She brought enchanted saddles. They can shrink down to child size just fine. They're intended for use with a flying horse, but they'd be okay on a grounded one too. Cute, but a bit predictable. *My* fiancé and I brought you—"

"Wait, what, *your* fiancé?" Dimitri stood up from the bed and charged around to their side of the room, his face going thundery. "Since when have you been engaged?"

Dyonne went all mushy. "It was all rather sudden. And romantic. And adventurous!"

"For both of us," Diana agreed. "In fact, it just happened. Whirlwind courtship, just like in romance novels. I thought for sure Kryptos would have spilled the beans." She nudged Dyonne.

"Kryptos?" Dimitri asked. "The weapons maker?"

Dyonne nodded. "That's my fiancé."

The mighty griffin who had faced down demons and death appeared as if he were about to fall over.

"Dimitri had his phone off," Diana reminded her sister. "Good thing."

Well, I was thrilled for them both. "Congratulations!" I gushed. I remembered Kryptos. He'd been Dyonne's childhood friend. He was a powerful griffin, a *rather* attractive man, and he was willing to put himself on the line when it counted. Dyonne could certainly do worse.

"He's so dreamy," she agreed. "And he's always said it's never too soon to get your kids used to sword fighting. Given your circumstances, he has a good point. Each of my nieces will have a set of enchanted swords, bucklers, and breastplates! They'll grow with the girls," she added proudly, "and the edges of the swords will be spelled to stay blunt when they spar each other until they turn eighteen."

"Oh my." They were going to turn my babies into Amazons straight out of the womb. "I—um—that's a good safety precaution."

Dyonne beamed. "I think so too!"

"They're both here?" Dimitri demanded. "Lurking outside with a car full of enchanted weapons and horse tack?"

Diana crossed her arms over her chest. "They're not lurking, they're being respectful of yours and Lizzie's privacy."

Dimitri squared his shoulders. "Well, they can respect me to my face and talk to me about this 'engagement' stuff at the same time. Lizzie"—he turned to look at me—"I'll be back in just a minute, all right?"

"I'm sure I'll be fine." I'd made it to the void and back. Family should be a piece of cake. Still, I didn't mind getting a little bit of breathing space. The more people crowded into this room, the hotter it felt. "Go talk with your sisters' fiancés. I'd like to see them again."

"Only after he vets them. Someone's had his overprotectiveness gene activated," Diana said with a sigh. "Lizzie, watch him, or you'll be lucky if your daughters are allowed to date by the time they're in their twenties."

Dimitri paused at the door. "More like thirty-five, I'm thinking," he said with a wink.

"I don't know if he's kidding or not," I said out loud.

But Dimitri didn't hear. He was already following his sisters out the door. "I never stopped you from dating!"

"Oh no?" Dyonne paused in the hall. "What about Niko?"

"Which Niko?" The twins followed Dimitri out of the room, and I went ahead and tilted the bed back a little farther. I really did feel pretty good now, just tired, like I could sleep for a week. I let my hand play across my stomach, wondering. When would I feel them move? Would I be able to tell one baby from the other?

"Hey, Lizzie!"

"Pirate!" I patted the bed, and he jumped up beside me, a fresh Sneak spell tucked into his collar. "Hey, buddy." I scratched him behind the ears. "Did you have a nice walk?"

He nudged my wrist with a nice, cold nose. "Oh, Lizzie, it was the best! There are so many critters around this hospital, and the trash cans all smell *really* intense." He let me work on his ears for another moment then turned and presented me with his butt and a hopeful look. I dutifully scratched right above his tail, and Pirate panted with joy.

"Where's Frieda?" I asked, surprised that she hadn't already come in.

"She stayed outside to have a cigarette, but she gave me a *super* important job!" He sounded proud. "I got to guide Philippa the Strange up to visit you! I bet I could be a guide dog, I'm so good at this stuff."

I was startled. "Wait, Philippa is here? Where?"

"Well, I'm not about to walk in without an invitation, am I?" a familiar voice groused from over by the door. "Not the way you've got this room sectioned off."

Grandma glanced up from a chair by the window, her eyes narrowing. "Tell her to piss off, Lizzie," she muttered.

"Bold words from a woman who needed my moly to pull her shit together," Philippa retorted.

"Come in," I said, happier than I had any right to be.

Philippa entered, her hair just as wild as before, but her overalls had been swapped out for a stiff, polyester dress in a floral print. It had to be decades old—it still had *shoulder pads*, for heaven's sake, and was nowhere near a match for the Birkenstocks on her feet. She carried a ceramic pot with a slender green stalk that ended in two tightly closed blossoms.

"Crazy Frieda got in touch just to let me know things turned out all right," Philippa said, blazing right past the pleasantries, pointedly ignoring Grandma. "Her timing was good. I figured I'd give you this before you run back off to California."

I didn't accept the plant she held out. The shoot appeared tender and new, the blossoms a snowy white. I did lean—but not too close. I didn't want it to bite my nose off or something. "What is it?"

"It's a variant of an angel orchid." Philippa set the pot on the bed next to me. "I treated it with your blood, fed a few spells in here and there, and now…it's completely unique. Only opens at the touch of a person with angel blood in them." She sounded proud.

Something clicked inside my head. "Is that why you asked for my blood?" She hadn't used it for power or control. "You just wanted to grow me a flower?"

"Is that a bad reason?" Philippa bristled. "It's about the most benign thing I can think of to use blood for, better than stuffing it in a spell jar and hurling it all over kingdom come."

Grandma practically growled. "Watch it, woman."

"Oh, go soak your head." Philippa focused back on the orchid. "Angel orchids are generally beautiful things, growing in all sorts of colors and shapes. Some look like flying angels, some like they're praying."

No kidding. "What do these ones look like?" I asked.

Philippa broke out into a grin. "I don't know. No angel blood in me." Her smile widened. "Why don't you touch it and find out?"

I glanced at Grandma, who nodded.

"Here goes nothing." I reached out with one finger and gently stroked the backs of the delicate blossoms. For a moment, nothing happened. Then bit by bit they began to unfurl, one layer of petals spreading like a pair of wings, the next uncoiling into a pair of tiny arms. A long, luxurious petal unfolded below the top two like a robe, all the petals swaying softly in an invisible breeze.

The flowers had started off pure white, but as I watched, a deep purple expanded from the heart of each one, overtaking the white until it was gone. Then the color changed to pink.

Then gold. Then a vibrant shade of orange. They were the colors I'd seen when my dad had come back to me—the colors of angels. After the amazing display, the flowers settled, bringing their petals back in close and nestling up together like…like…

I glanced over at the picture that Grandma still held in her hands. Two babies nestled together inside me. Two blossoms, just the same.

"Oh, Philippa." It was too much. "They're beautiful."

"They'll always bloom in pairs," Philippa said quietly, her eyes still rapt on the orchid.

Amazing. "What else do the flowers do?" I asked. I'd never seen anything like it.

Philippa blinked and shook her head. "Nothing else. They exist, and they are lovely. What else *should* a flower do?"

Well, after hanging out with the biker witches all these years, I never could tell. "No angel fire?" I prompted. "No weaponized scent? No razor petals?"

"Ah, Lizzie." Philippa patted my hand. "You're going to have very special, very powerful children who will be given many special and powerful things and be expected to use them for all sorts of reasons. It doesn't hurt to have something around that lives just for the sake of living and is beautiful without needing to be more. Do you understand me?"

I finally think I did. "Yes," I replied, turning my hand over and giving hers a squeeze. "I *do* understand you. And it is an incredible gift."

EPILOGUE

A year and seven months later, we gathered again in my mother's cream-on-white living room to celebrate the twins' first birthday.

You could tell where Rory had been by the festive pink smear left behind on the carpet. Of the twins, Rory was the more mobile one—getting her to sit still and eat one of Hillary's gorgeous, way-too-elaborate birthday cupcakes was a losing proposition. Instead, the dark-haired, olive-skinned little girl triumphantly squashed the icing between her fingers and then took off for the back porch at the run-fall-run-fall pace that was her trademark right now.

"She gets that from Dimitri," I said to my mom.

But she wasn't listening.

"Aurora!" Hillary called after her. "Wait for Grammy, honey!" She left without a second glance at the floor, which was practically a miracle. Heaven knew *I'd* have gotten an earful if I made such a mess as a child.

I stayed on the couch and shared a glance with Grandma. "It's like Mom's had a personality transplant where the kids are concerned," I said, still turning over my parents' gift for the girls in my hands. It was a Baby Genius thingamajig—one of those toys that came with lights, music, and various tactile accessories meant "To Start Your Baby On The Path To Learning!" At least that was what the box promised. Personally, I thought we'd be lucky if it lasted a week of the twins' very robust affections.

"Eh, why should she worry?" my grandma said from where she lounged with Helena on her lap, who was more sedately eating a tiny cupcake of her own. Helena had my coloring, and she liked to stay neat most of the time. She wore a flowered dress, along with Grandma's birthday present to her, a denim vest with a red skull emblazoned on the back of it, and astonishingly, it was still mostly acid-wash blue and not icing colored. "The Sweeper spell is gonna clean it up anyway."

The Sweeper spell was one of a dozen new magical inventions the witches had invented after the babies were born. It was a flat, squishy thing that worked like a mystical Roomba, trailing after whoever was making a mess and sucking it into the ether.

It worked great—too great, sometimes. We'd had to have Grandma put some limitations on it after Pirate woke up one morning with the Sweeper on his head, casually sucking out "all the smells that make me me!"

They'd been archenemies ever since.

Speaking of Pirate... He sat attentively at Grandma's feet, whispering up at Helena, "Just a few crumbs! Good, perfect! Now, see that globby bit there on your hand? Push it off with your—yes—yes—*you're so close*—"

"No begging the babies for food." It had become his favorite pastime.

He looked at me with a hangdog expression. "But, Lizzie, if I don't get it, that *smell thief* will!"

"No, it won't." It really wouldn't, because Helena had apparently just decided she was done with eating politely and mashed the entire thing against her face with a cry of glee.

The cupcake oozed off after a second, leaving a baby-nose

imprint in what was left of the icing as it fell to the ground. Pirate snarfed it up before I could utter a word, then hightailed it out of the living room with a "Thanks, Lenny!"

Grandma cackled. She held Helena out to me. "Mom's turn to take her."

I'd noticed that it was usually only my turn to hold the twins when they were messy, smelly or crying. When they were being perfect angels, everyone else wanted a go. Frieda had even started using nicotine patches on the days we got together so she wouldn't reek of smoke around the babies.

I got up off the couch and took Helena, who grinned widely at me. I grinned back—it was impossible not to. "Let's get you cleaned up, huh?" As much as I like the Sweeper, I wasn't letting that thing anywhere near my kiddo's face.

"I've got her, Lizzie," a sultry voice murmured.

I turned around just in time for Dimitri to sidle up to me and press a kiss to my cheek as he reached for Helena. "You wiped off the last round of food."

"True." Bananas didn't have the staining power of frosting, but boy, did they get everywhere. I leaned in and kissed his lips. "Thank you." Then I kissed him again, just for good measure. Then again…

Sticky hands pawed at our faces, and Dimitri pulled back with a chuckle. "Feeling neglected?" he asked our older daughter. Older by three minutes, but according to Diana and Dyonne, it still counted. "Let me fix that." He carried her off to the nearest bathroom, and I headed to the backyard to check on everyone else.

The twins' first birthday party looked like a roaring success. I leaned a hip against the frame of the kitchen door and looked out at the lawn. Creely had set up a—what had she called it, a trebuchet? Mangonel? Whatever it was, it flung chestnuts at floating balloons spelled to look like the witches' ex boyfriends, and all the witches were taking potshots at them and making bets.

Nearby, the garden was in full bloom. Yet I could see the angel statue my parents had installed shortly after my dad's death. Close to it, in a bed of forget-me-nots, stood a small cement Red Skull.

A firm hand clapped me on the back, and I turned to see my mentor, Rachmort. He'd been out of purgatory for a few months now and had good color from the last two months on the beach in Boca Raton. "You did good, kid." He smiled, his cheeks red and his white Einstein hair wild about his face.

"I had help," I said, not only from his training, but from my friends, my family.

He raised a frosted copper glass, the watch on his gold waistcoat jingling against a gold button. "I'm gonna grab another one of these. Heaven knows what's in it."

"If it's Hillary, it's top-shelf," I told him. "If it's the Red Skulls…"

"Anything goes." He grinned and headed jauntily out into the yard to join the others.

Hillary worked her way around and between her guests with a tray of amuse-bouches, probably bacon-wrapped dates from the way Ant Eater was trailing along behind her, eating one for every two Hillary passed out.

Frieda chatted in the shade with Philippa, who, I was a little surprised had responded to the invitation. She wore a long flowered dress and appeared to be asking questions about the nicotine patches dotting Frieda's arm.

Baby Rory entertained Cliff over by the gazebo. Cliff had icing all across the front of his shirt, but he didn't even seem to notice. He had Rory perched on his hip, and he was doing the gentle bounce-bounce-bounce that seemed to be a requirement when it came to holding little kids like it was second nature. Rory and Flappy were cooing at each other, Flappy's tail twitching back and forth in dragonly delight.

My parents really had been transformed by the babies. We

all had. My family was larger and more loving than ever now, and I'd never been happier.

I felt Dimitri before I saw him, one hand trailing up my spine and coming to rest on my shoulder as he joined me at the door. He held Helena in his arms. She was clean as could be without completely changing her outfit. She smiled a gap-toothed grin at me, and I ruffled her soft, dark hair.

The girls looked so much like me and their daddy. I couldn't wait to see how they turned out—whether their aunt Diana would get one of them interested in flying horses, whether they'd have the aptitude I lacked for casting spells. Whether they'd embrace their heritage as demon slayers or fight it like my mother, and even like I had for a while.

For now though, I was content just to lean into my husband's caress, kiss my closest kiddo on the head, and watch the birthday party roll on. "I love this," I told him. "You, the girls, my parents, the coven…it's everything I never knew I wanted. I feel spoiled."

"Cherish that feeling while you can," Dimitri replied knowingly. "Because, babe…you're up next on diaper duty."

I snorted a laugh before I could stifle it. "Great, thanks for the reminder."

He leaned in and kissed me. "Anything for you, Lizzie."

And he meant it, too.

NOTE FROM ANGIE FOX

Thank you so much for joining me on this crazy, magical journey with Lizzie and the gang. This is the first series I ever wrote, the one that started as a scribbled idea on the back of a Macy's envelope and blossomed into a series spanning ten years. That said, this will be the last demon slayer book. I've loved writing each and every book. And heaven knows, the witches are going to make interesting babysitters, but I've decided to concentrate on other books for now.

Thank you for the love and support you've shown this series. I've read every one of your letters and emails. I have your character illustrations hanging in my office. There's nothing like the Red Skulls, Pirate, Flappy, Dimitri, and Lizzie getting together for an adventure and for that, I am truly grateful.

—Angie

ABOUT THE AUTHOR

New York Times and *USA Today* bestselling author Angie Fox writes sweet, fun, action-packed mysteries. Her characters are clever and fearless, but in real life, Angie is afraid of basements, bees, and going up stairs when it's dark behind her. Let's face it: Angie wouldn't last five minutes in one of her books.

Angie earned a journalism degree from the University of Missouri. During that time, she also skipped class for an entire week so she could read Anne Rice's vampire series straight through. Angie has always loved books and is shocked, honored and tickled pink that she now gets to write books for a living. Although, she did skip writing for a week this past fall so she could read Lynsay Sands's Argeneau vampire series straight through.

Angie makes her home in St. Louis, Missouri with a football-addicted husband, two kids, and Moxie the dog.

If you are interested in receiving an email each time Angie releases a new book, please sign up at www.angiefox.com.

Also be sure to join Angie's online Facebook community where you will find contests, quizzes and special sneak peeks of new books.

Connect with Angie Fox online:
www.angiefox.com
angie@angiefox.com

72130024R00132

Made in the USA
Middletown, DE
03 May 2018